There are way too many unicorn
stories, so this book will be
a unicorn-free zone.
And it will be set where you
definitely won't find unicorns –
THE WILD WEST!

For Bonnie, love Dad - F.B.

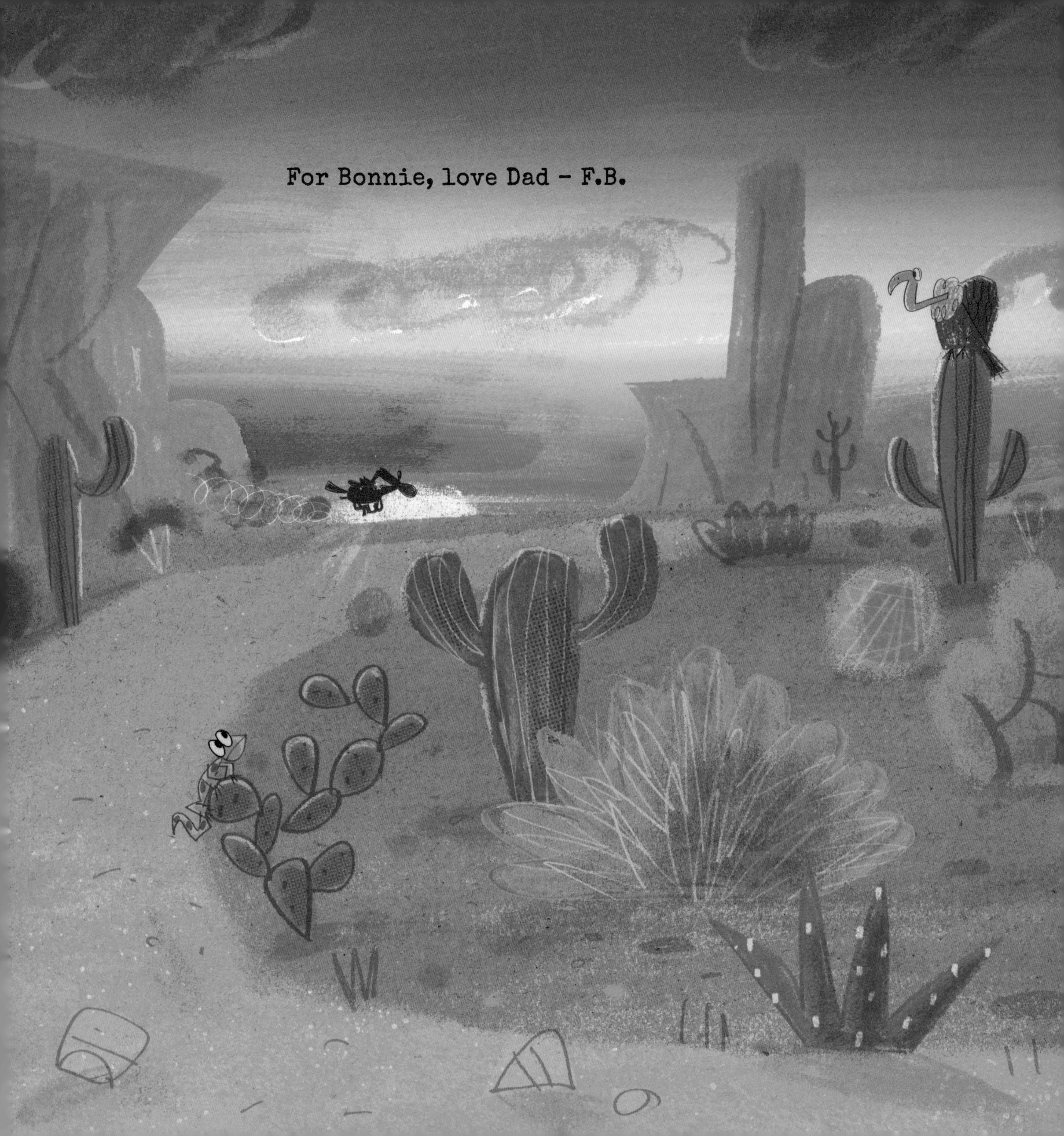

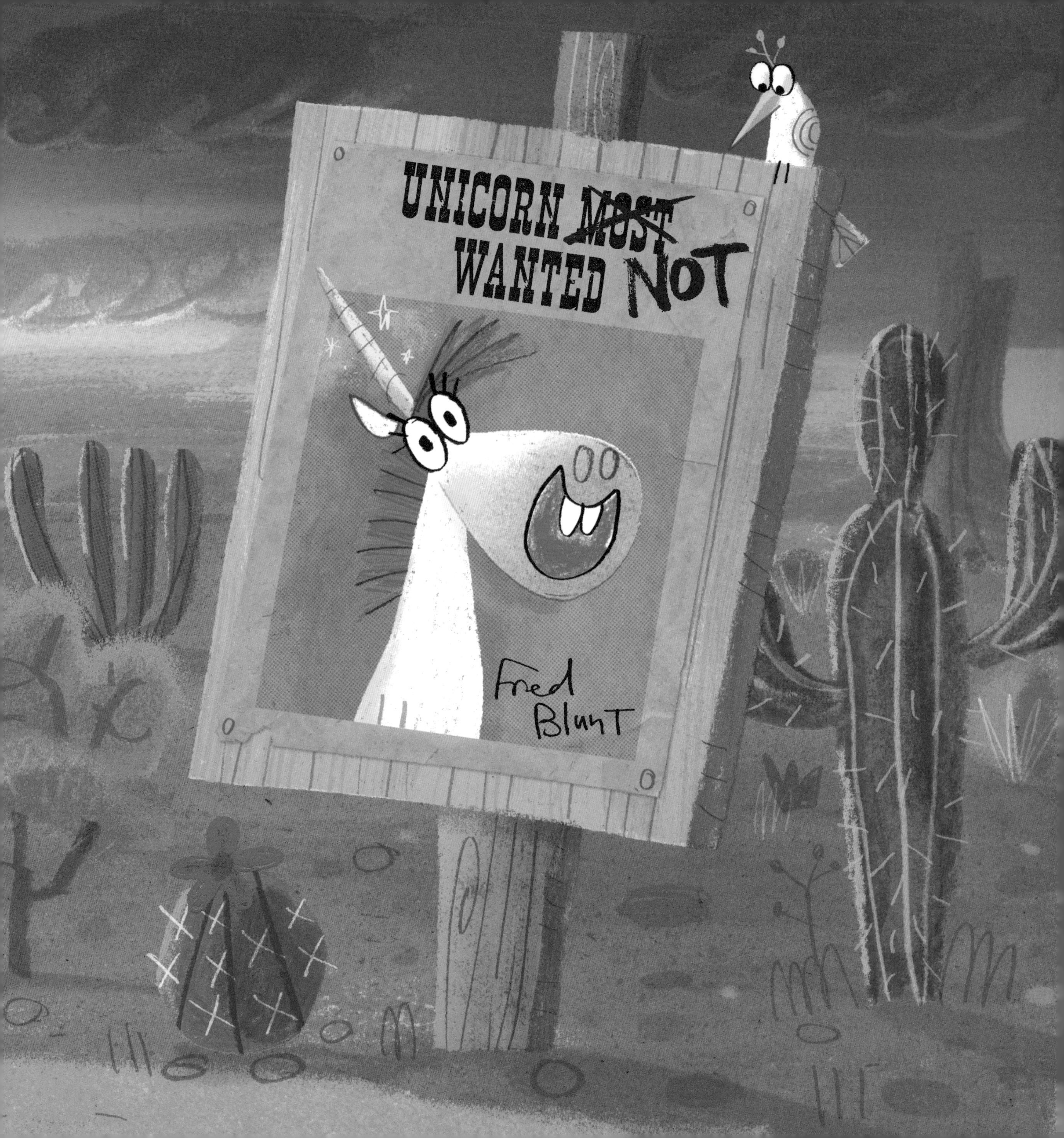
UNICORN MOST
WANTED NOT
Fred
Blunt

WELCOME

to this exciting story of...

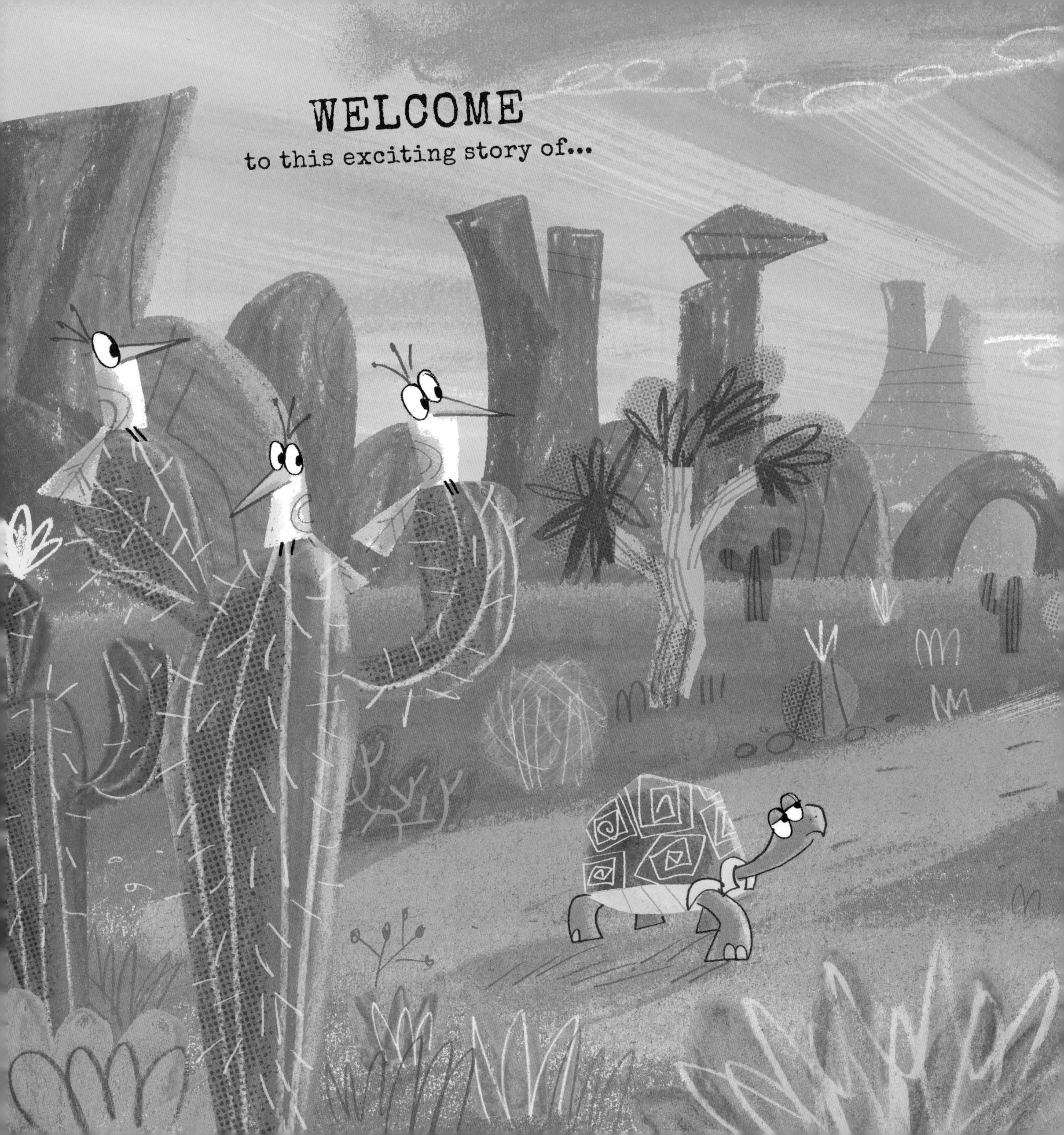

ADVENTURE,
DRAMA,
ACTION and...

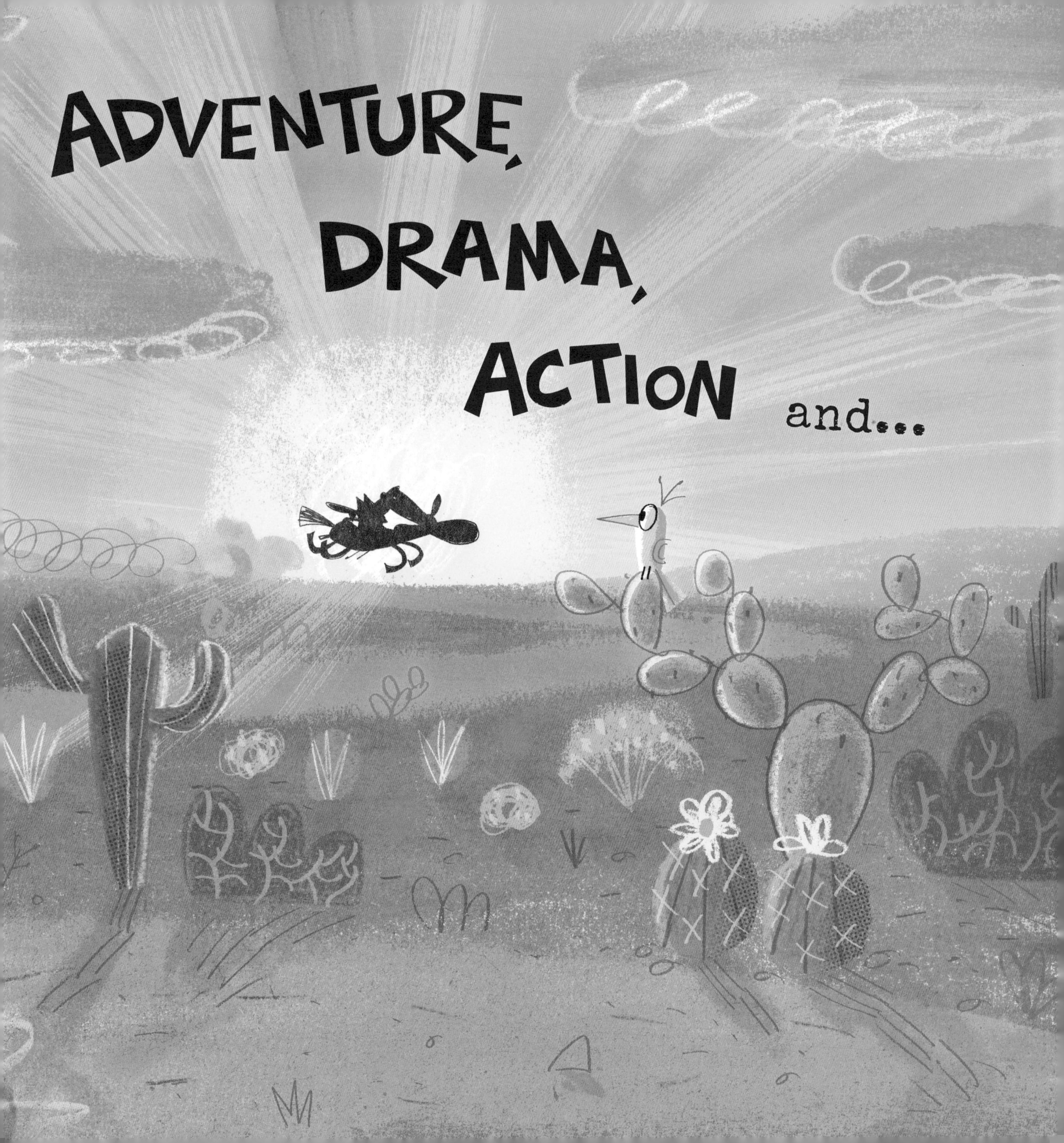

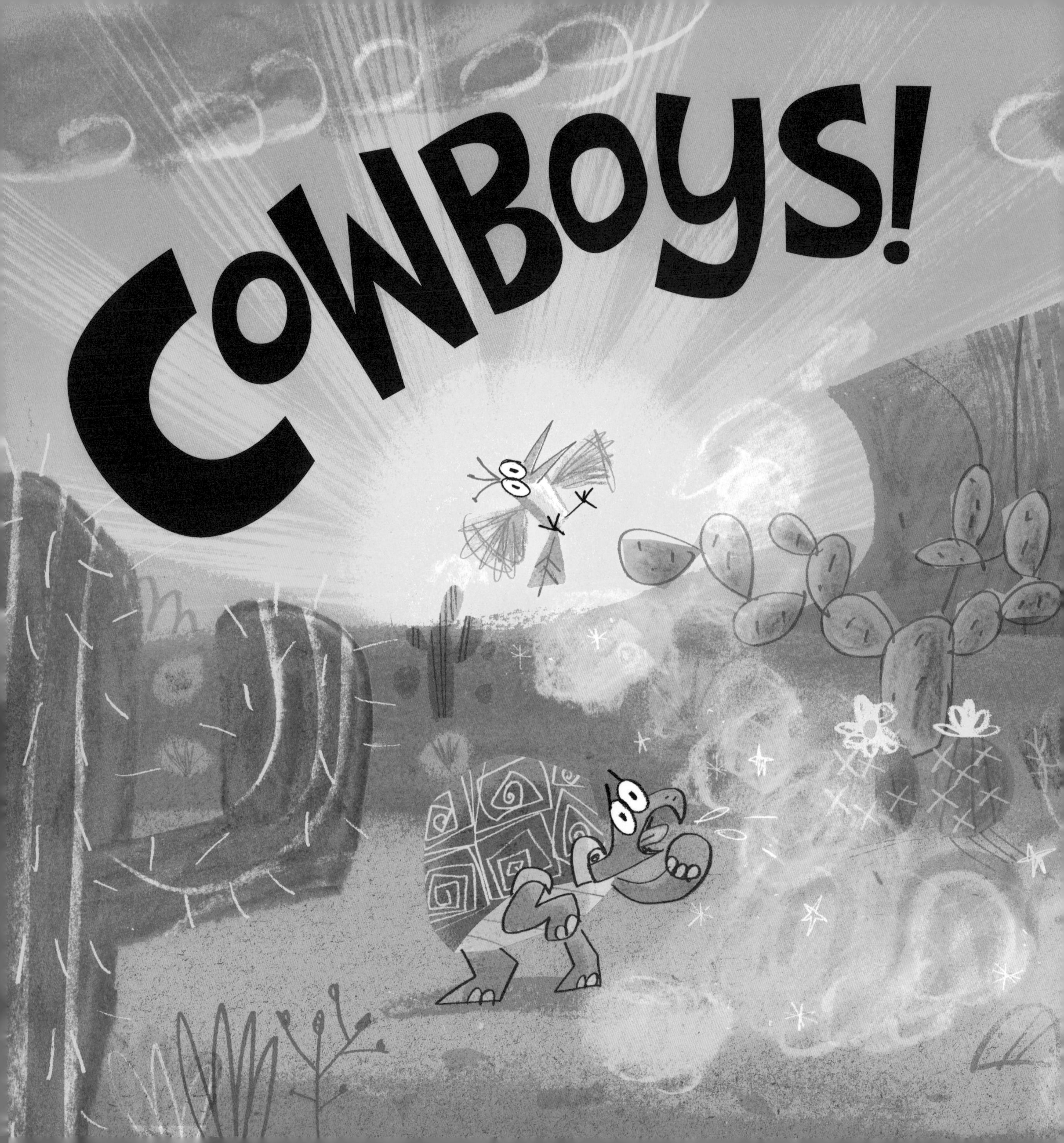
COWBOYS!

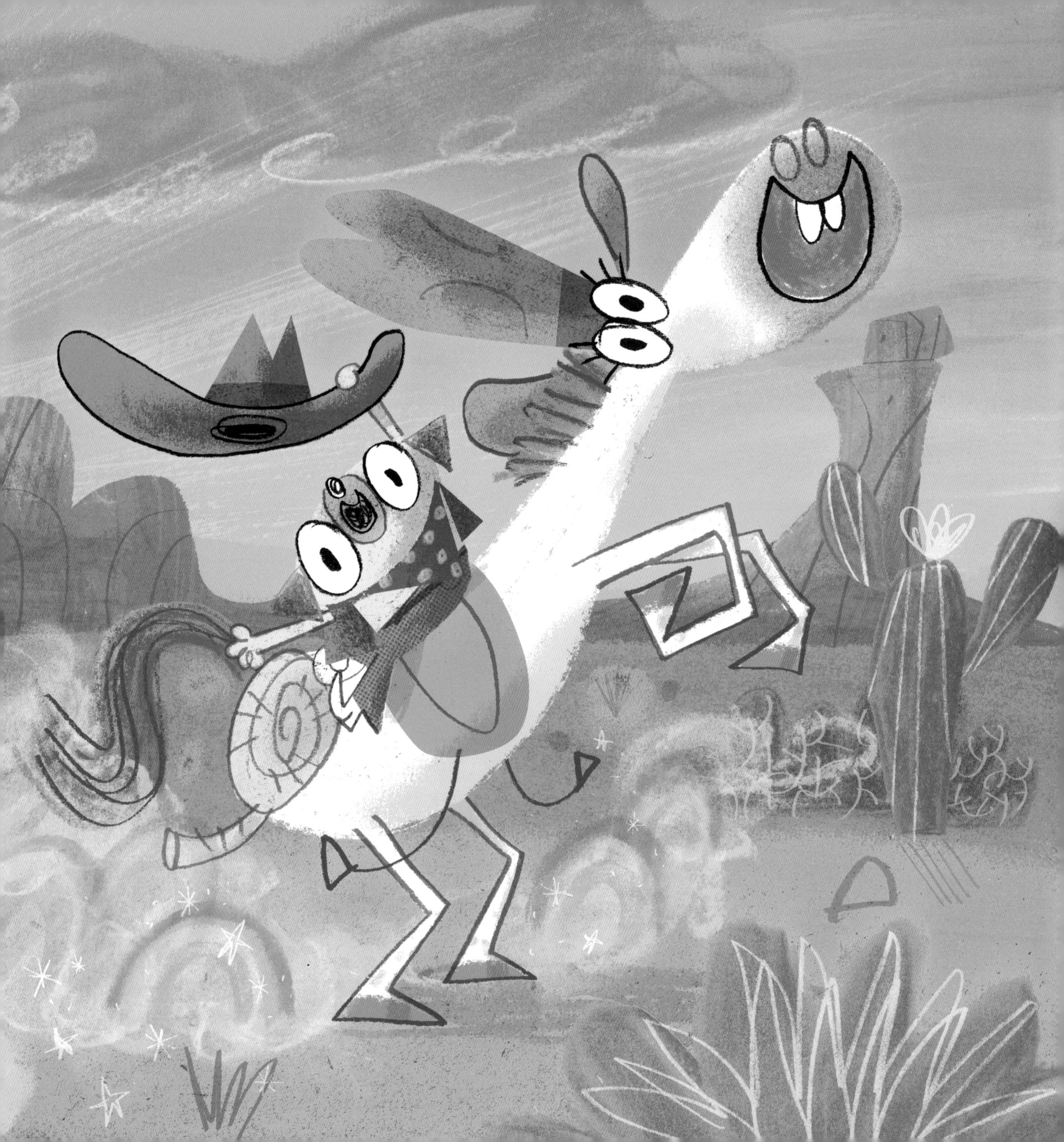

Wait a minute.

That's not a cowboy...

that's a pug!

And why is that horse wearing such a tall hat?

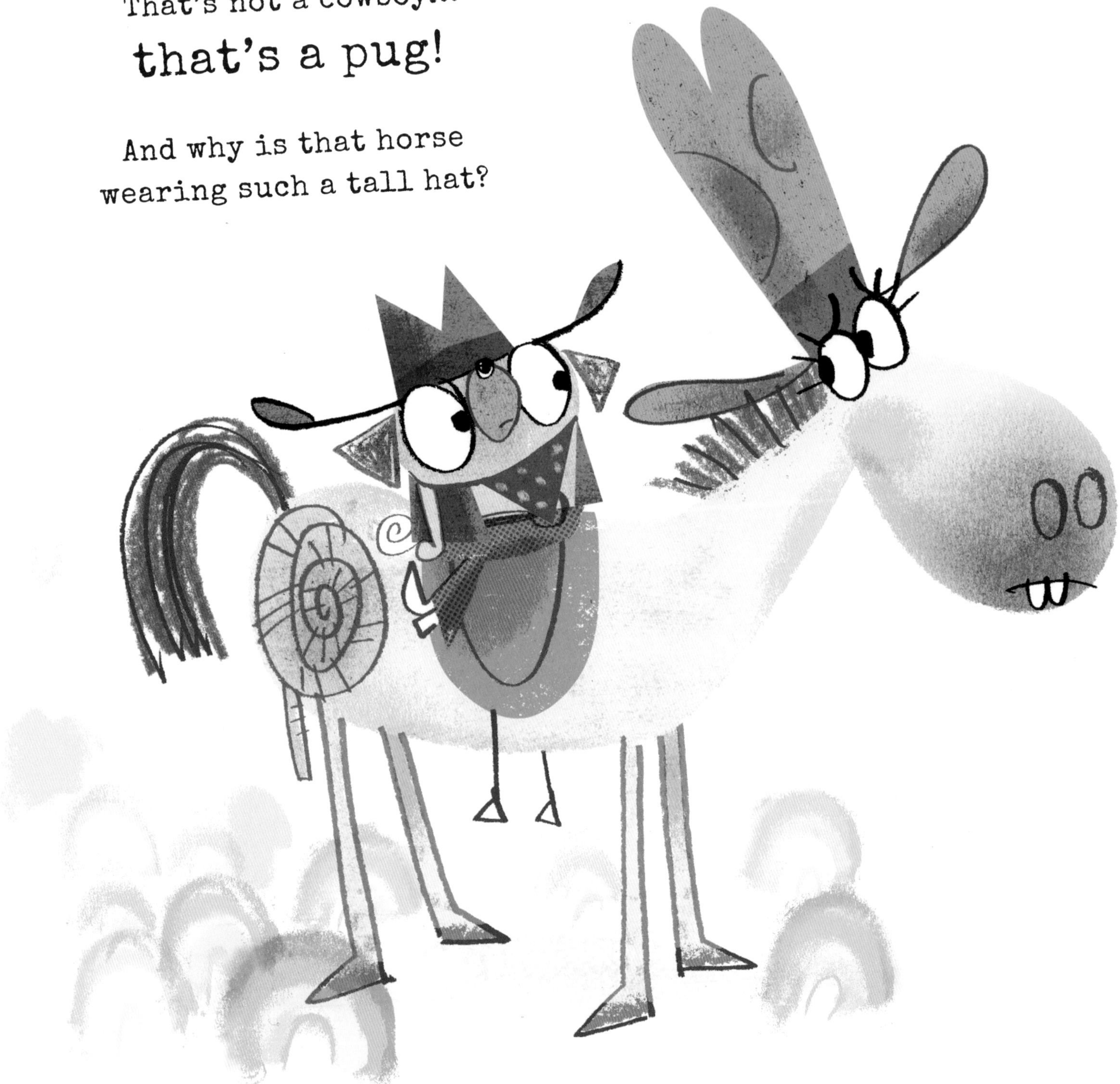

Right, that's enough –
lift up the horse's hat
please, pug.

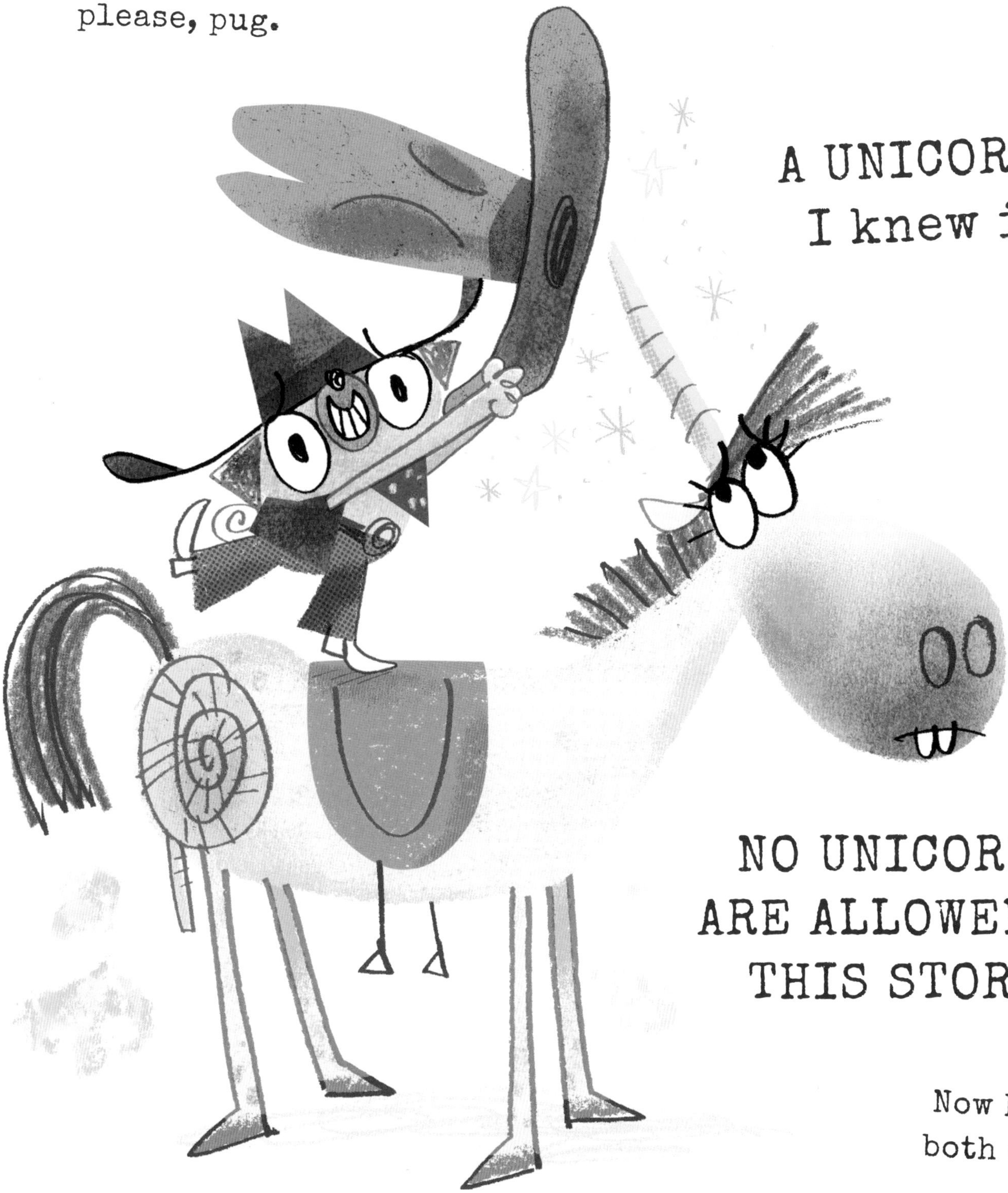

A UNICORN –
I knew it!

NO UNICORNS
ARE ALLOWED IN
THIS STORY!

Now hop it,
both of you.

Sorry for that interruption.

Now, let's get back to our cowboy story and meet the sheriff and his deputy.

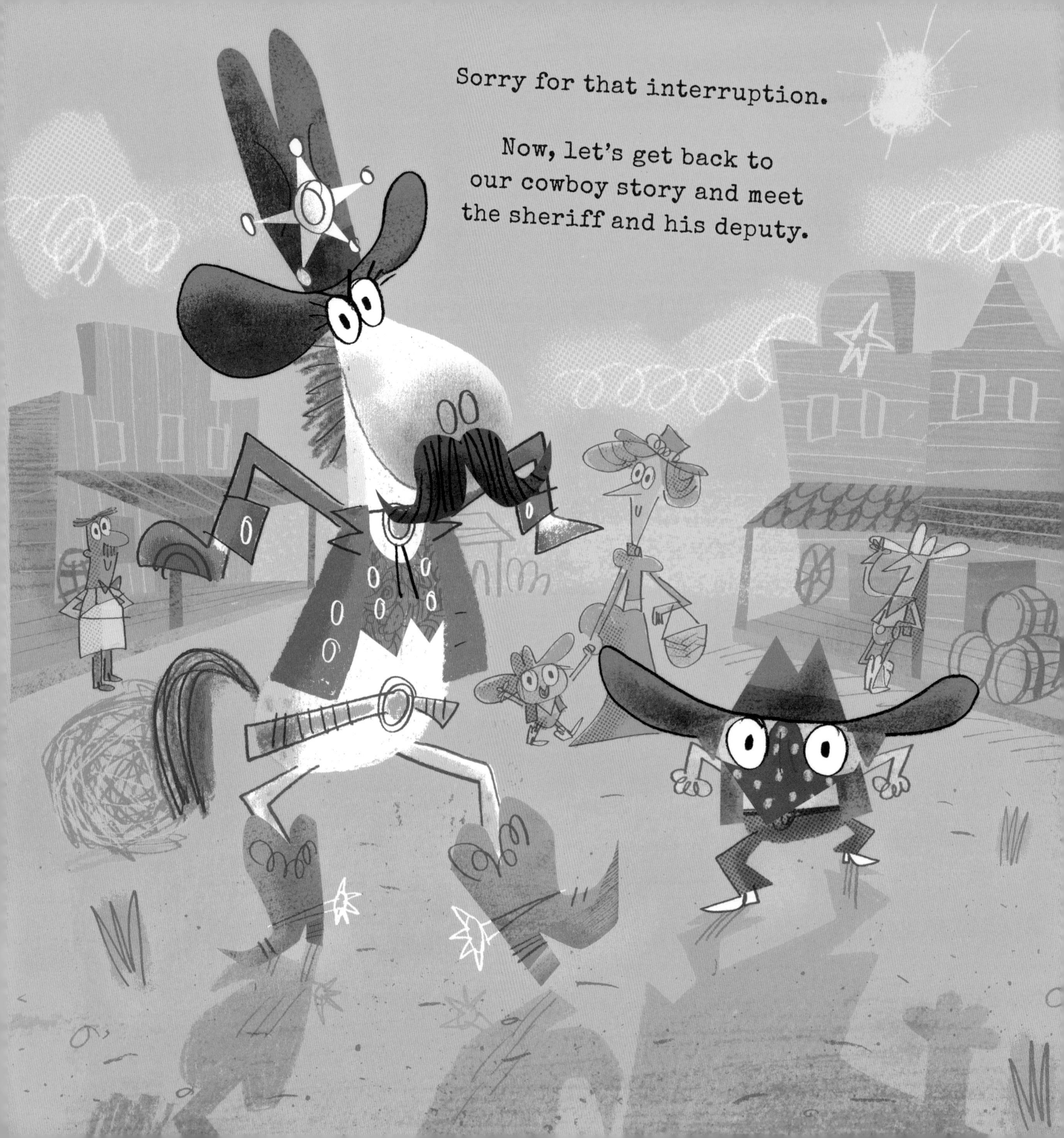

Hold on.
You two look familiar...

Take off that silly
moustache and scarf.

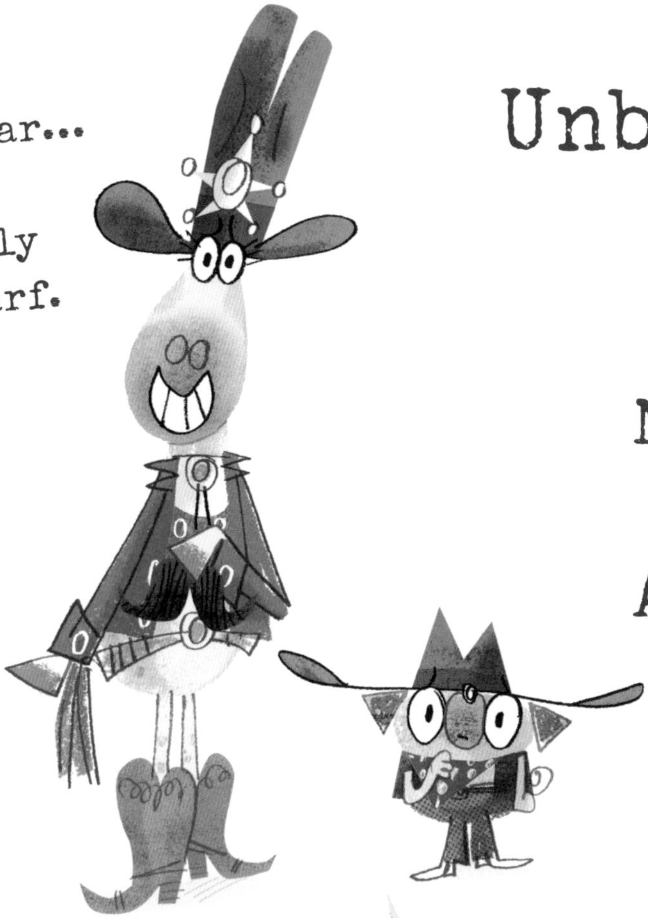

Unbelievable!

There are
NO,
I repeat,
NO unicorns
in this story.

And no pugs
either!

Now please
leave,
once and for all.

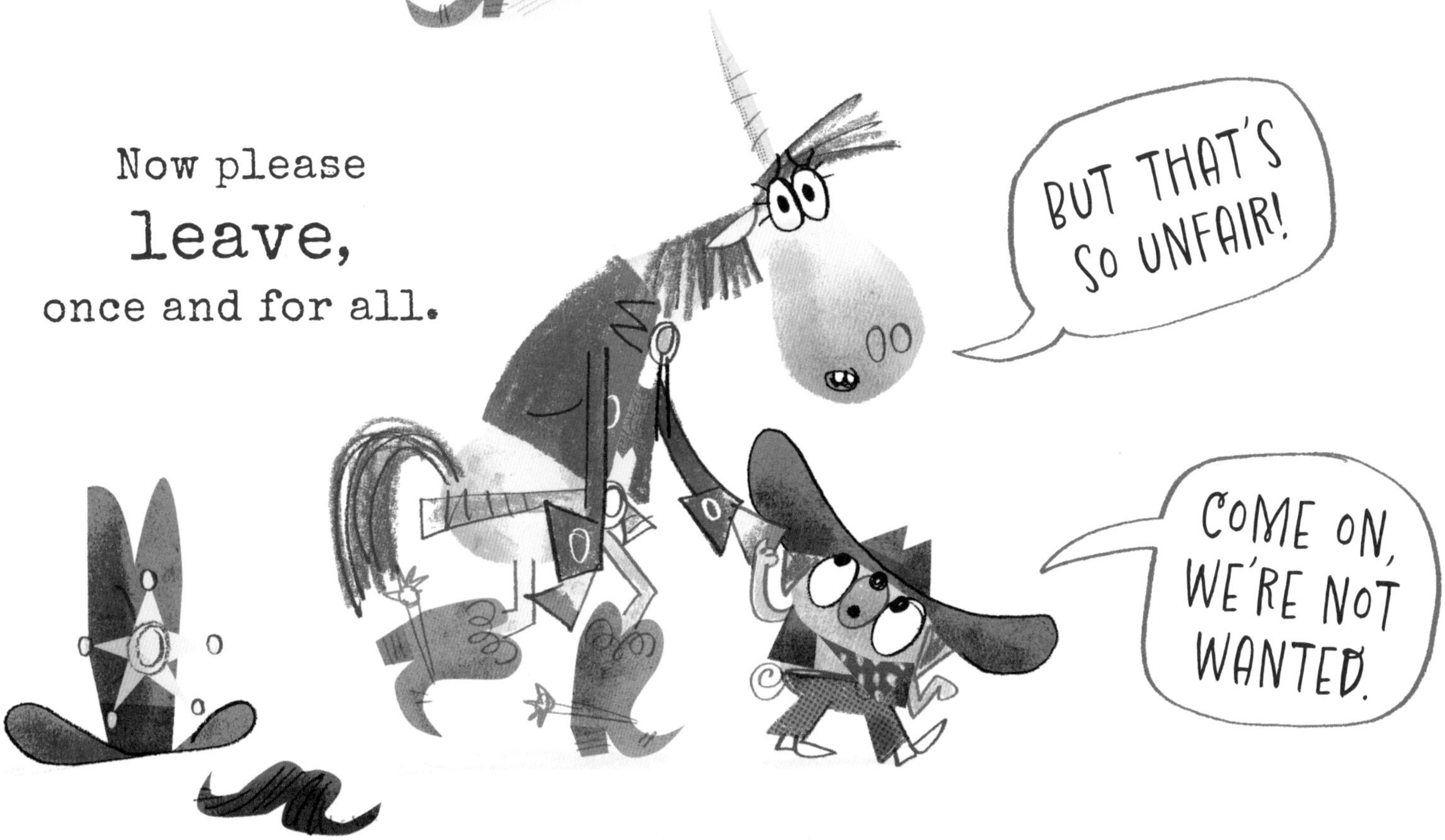
BUT THAT'S SO UNFAIR!
COME ON, WE'RE NOT WANTED.

Now, where were we?
Ah yes, back to our exciting
story about...

No, not about sniff, about...

SNIFF
SNIFF

What on earth is that sniffing?

YOU'RE MAKING HER CRY!

You're ruining the story.
Keep it down, please.

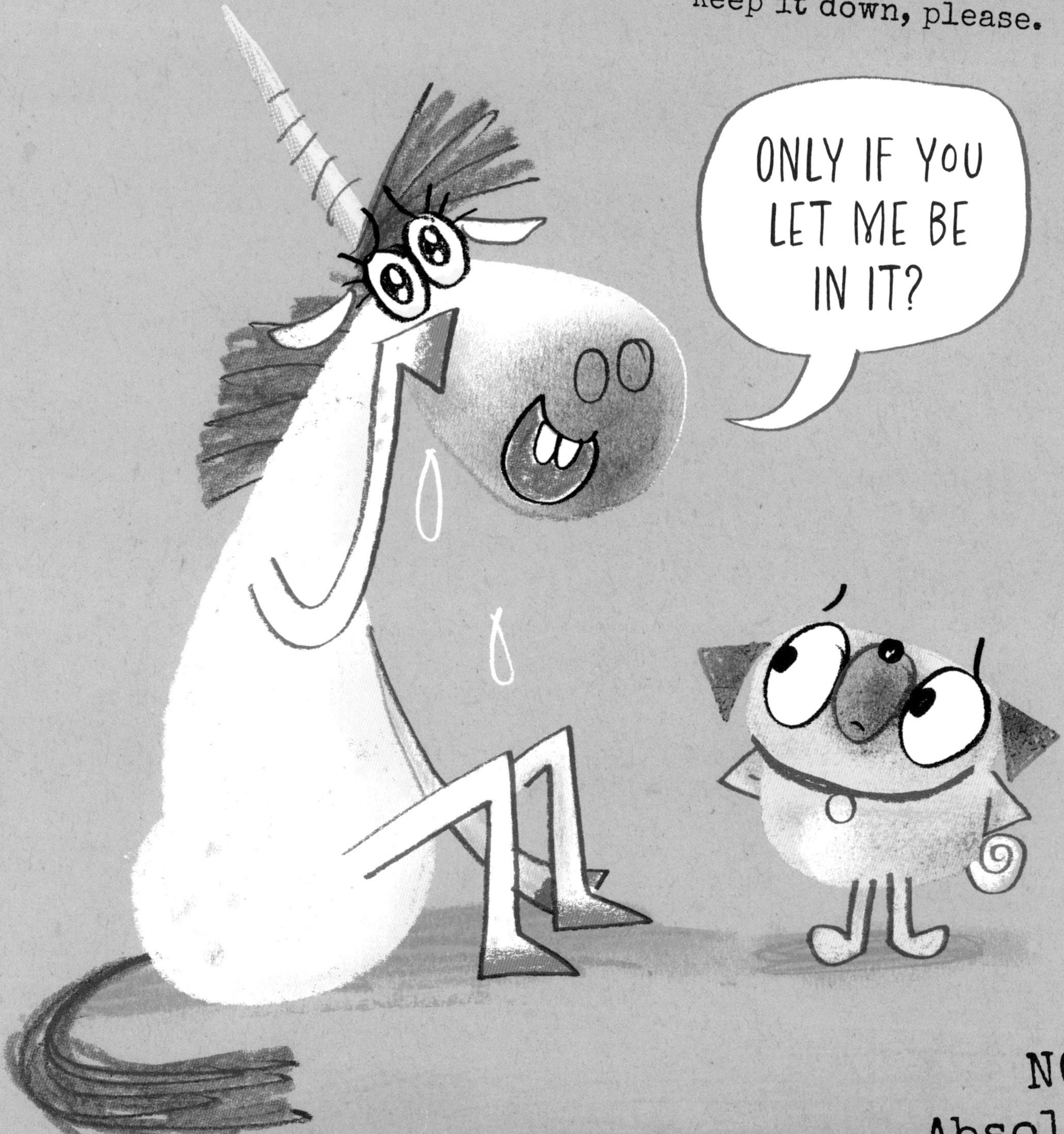
ONLY IF YOU LET ME BE IN IT?

NO!
Absolutely
not.

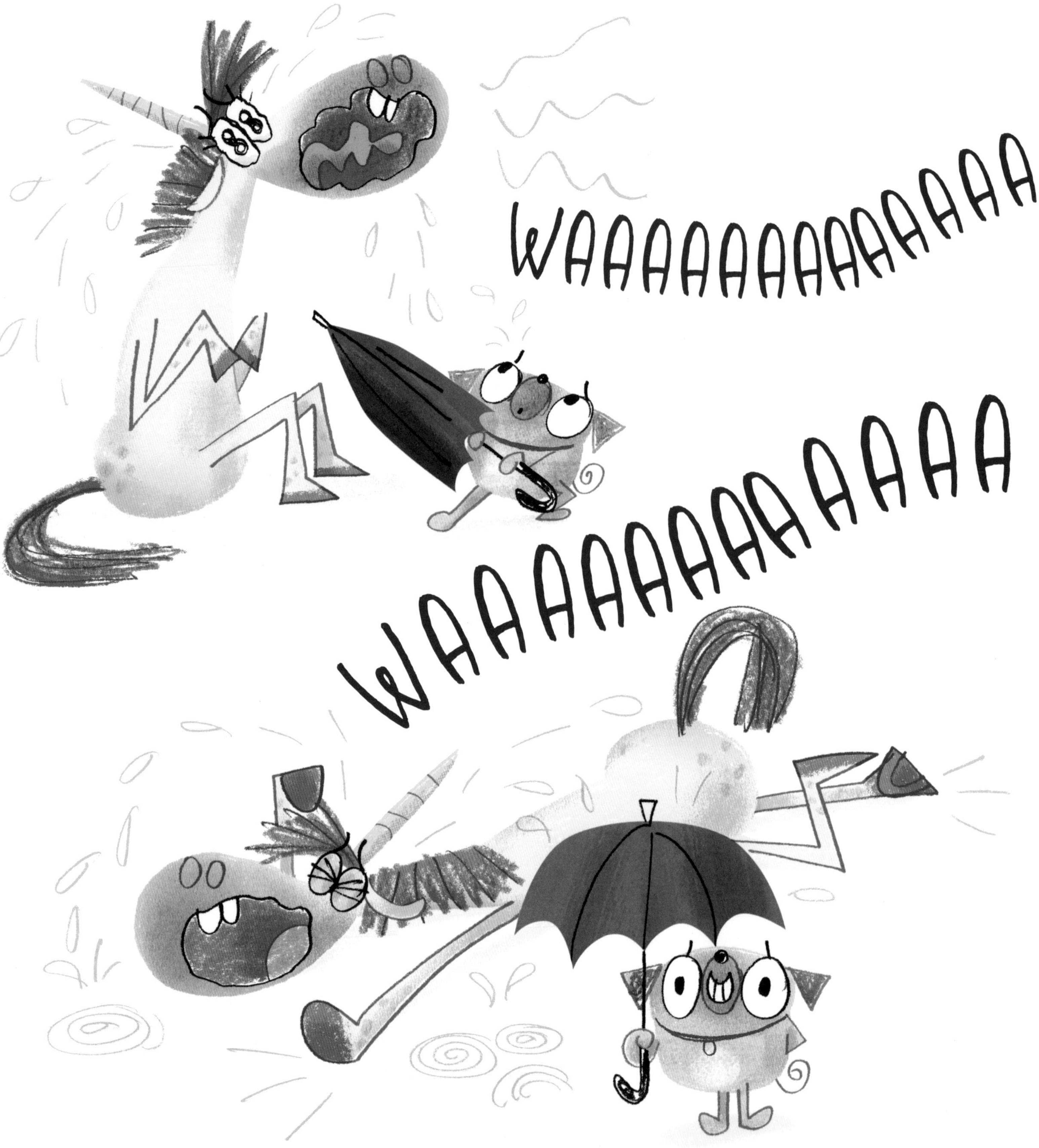
WAAAAAAAAAAAAA
WAAAAAAAAAAAAA

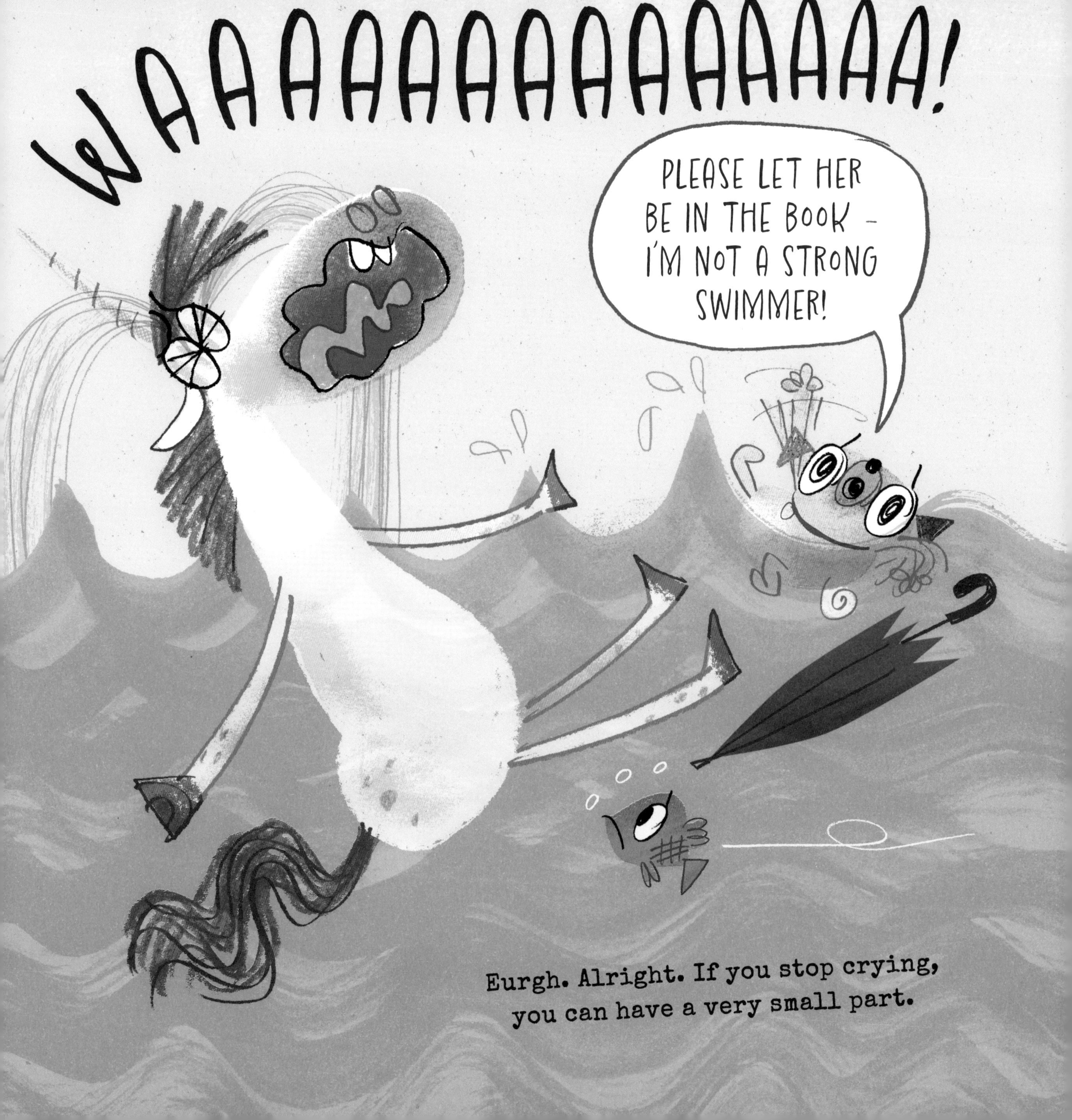
WAAAAAAAAAAAAAA!
PLEASE LET HER BE IN THE BOOK – I'M NOT A STRONG SWIMMER!

Eurgh. Alright. If you stop crying,
you can have a very small part.

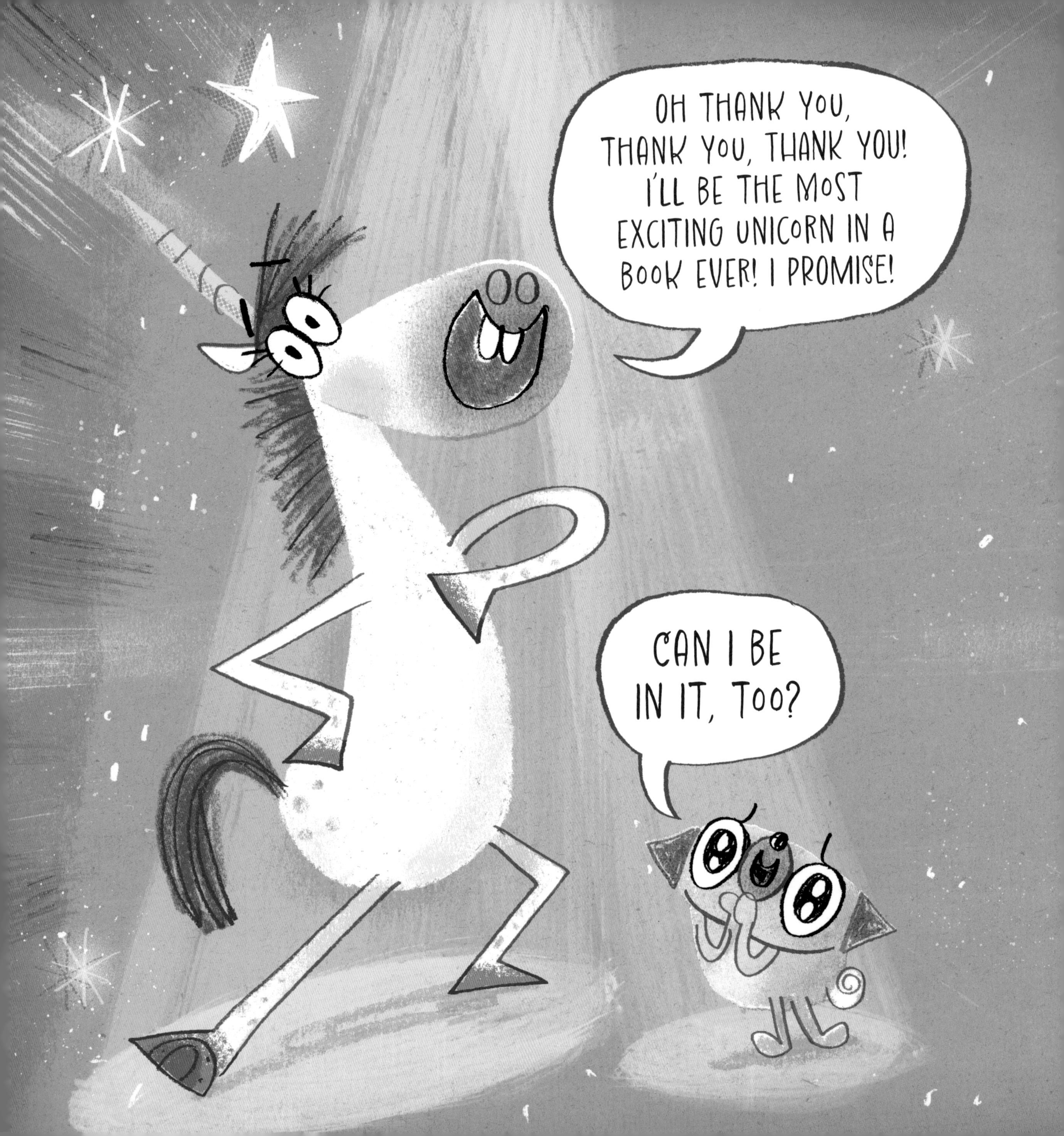
OH THANK YOU, THANK YOU, THANK YOU! I'LL BE THE MOST EXCITING UNICORN IN A BOOK EVER! I PROMISE!
CAN I BE IN IT, TOO?

If you must.
Just don't be loud,
don't take up too much
space and don't get
too excited. Deal?

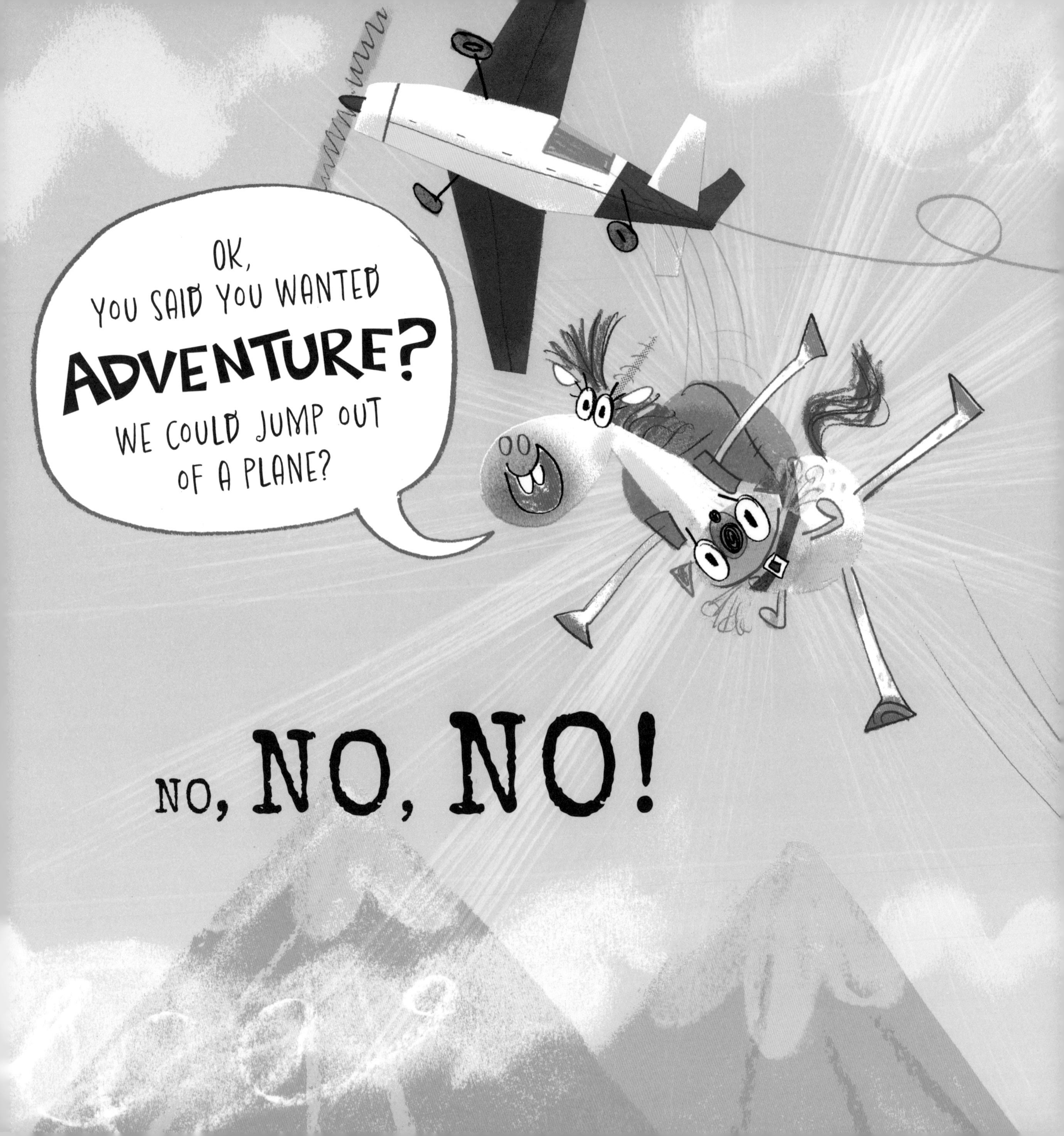
OK, YOU SAID YOU WANTED ADVENTURE? WE COULD JUMP OUT OF A PLANE?

NO, NO, NO!

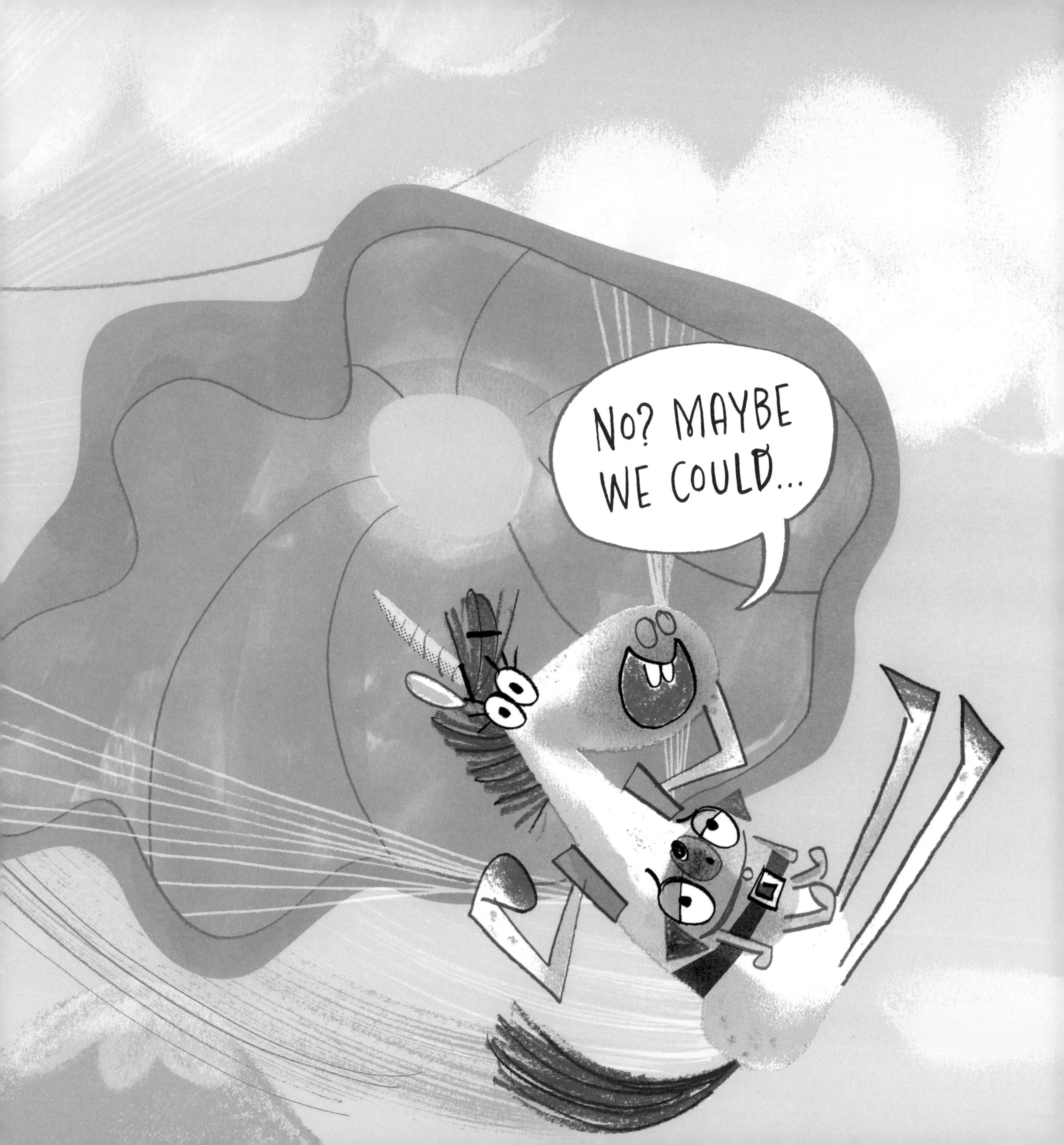
NO? MAYBE WE COULD...

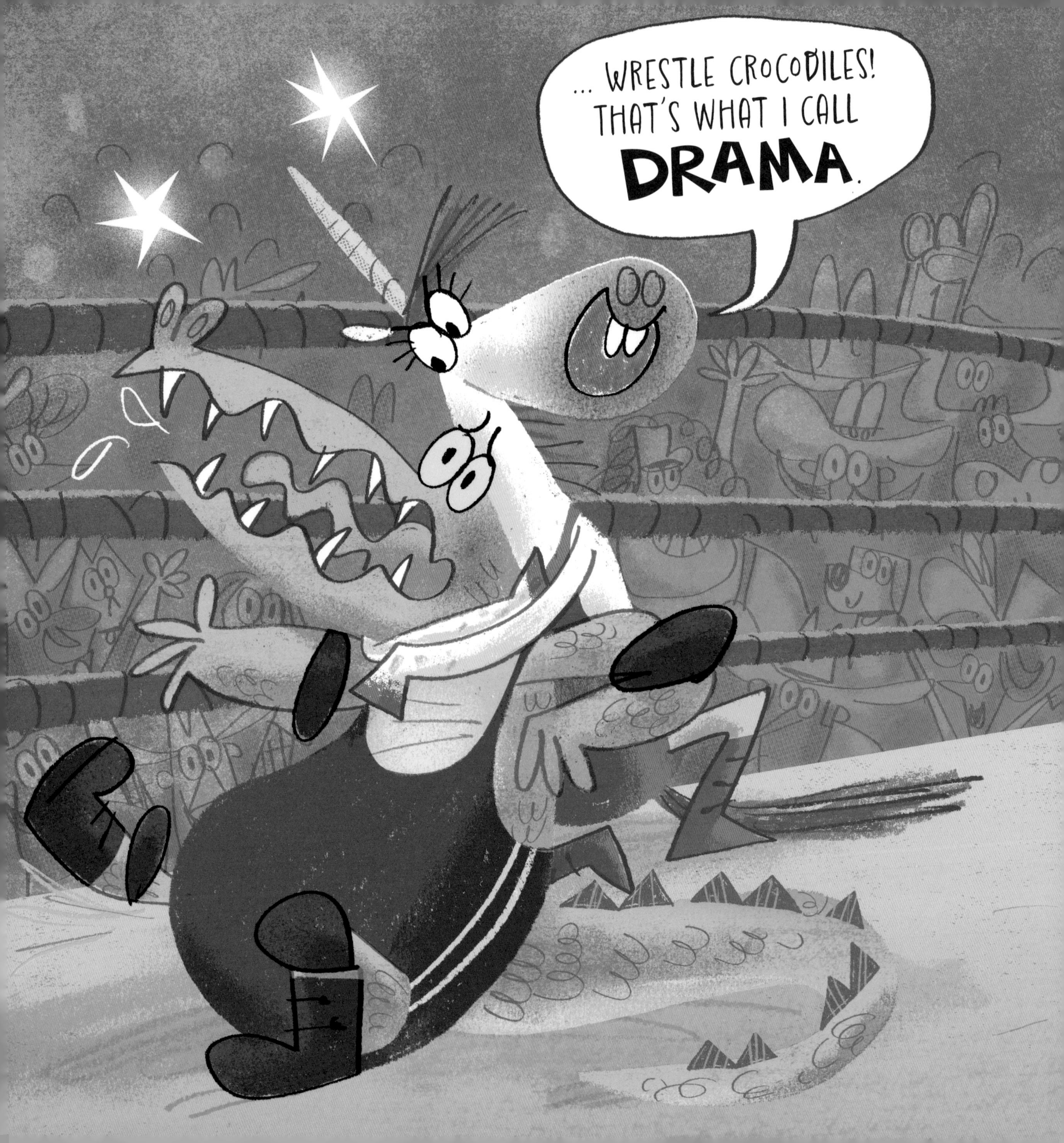
... WRESTLE CROCODILES! THAT'S WHAT I CALL DRAMA.

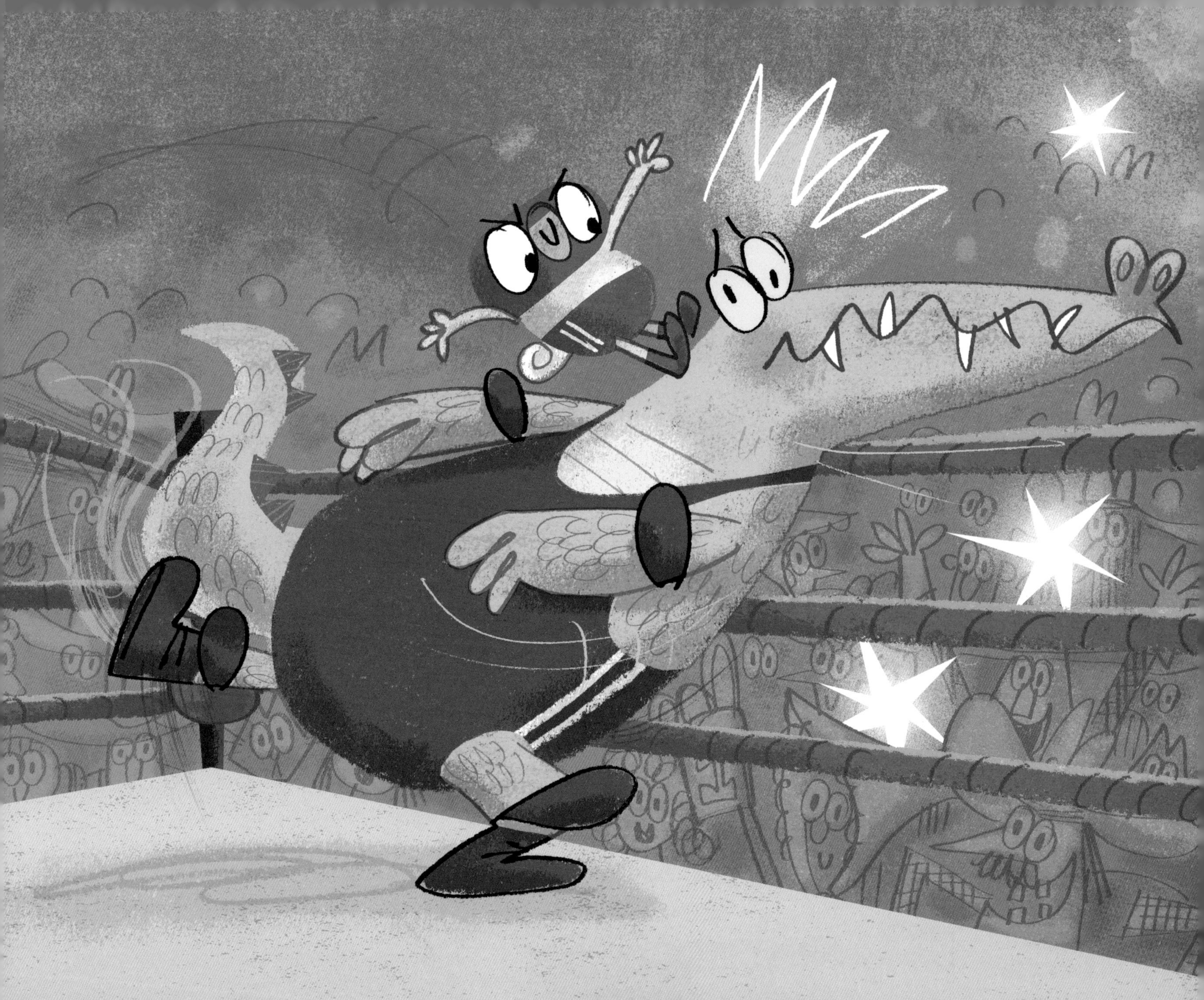

I SAID **NO...**

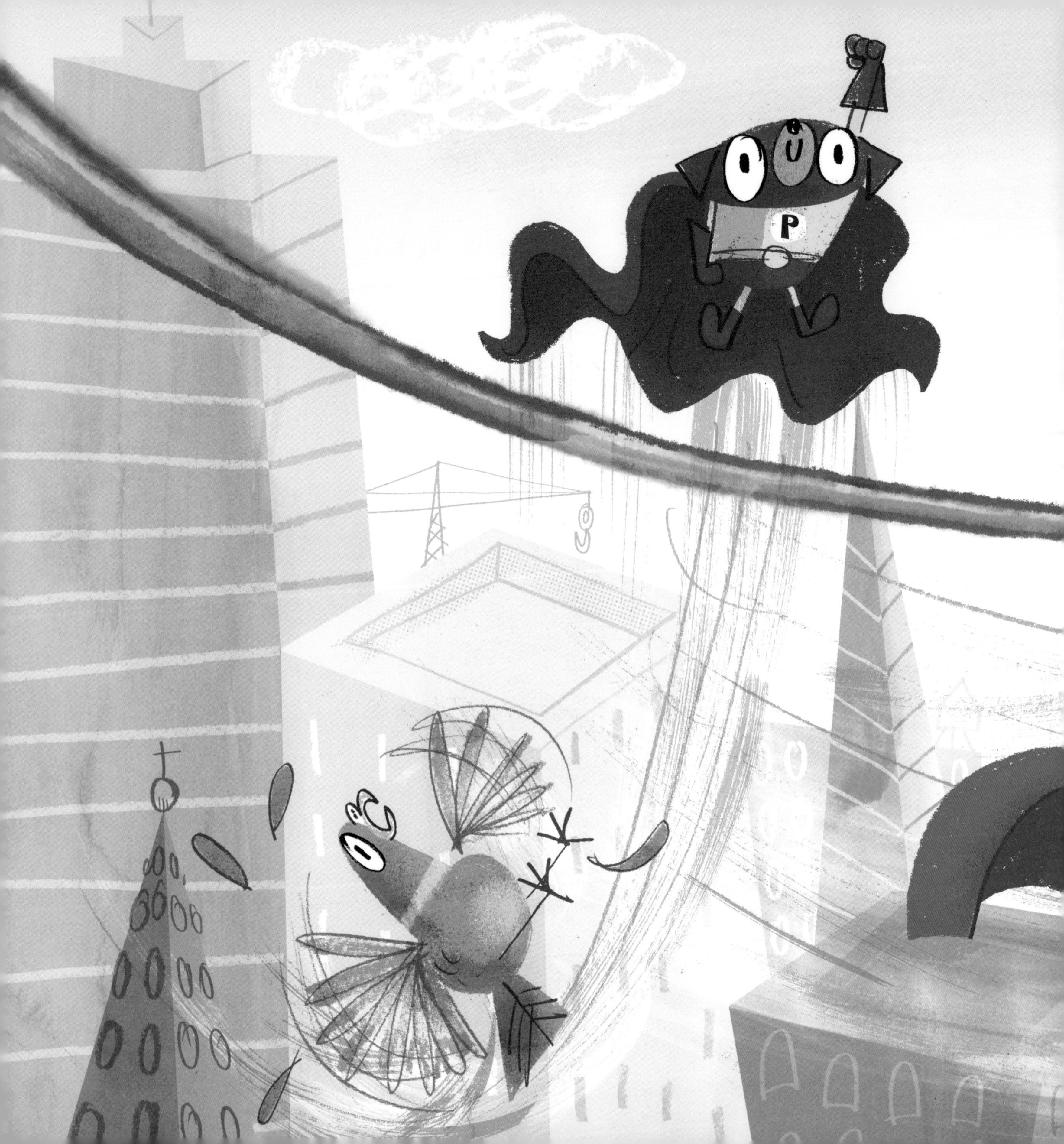
P

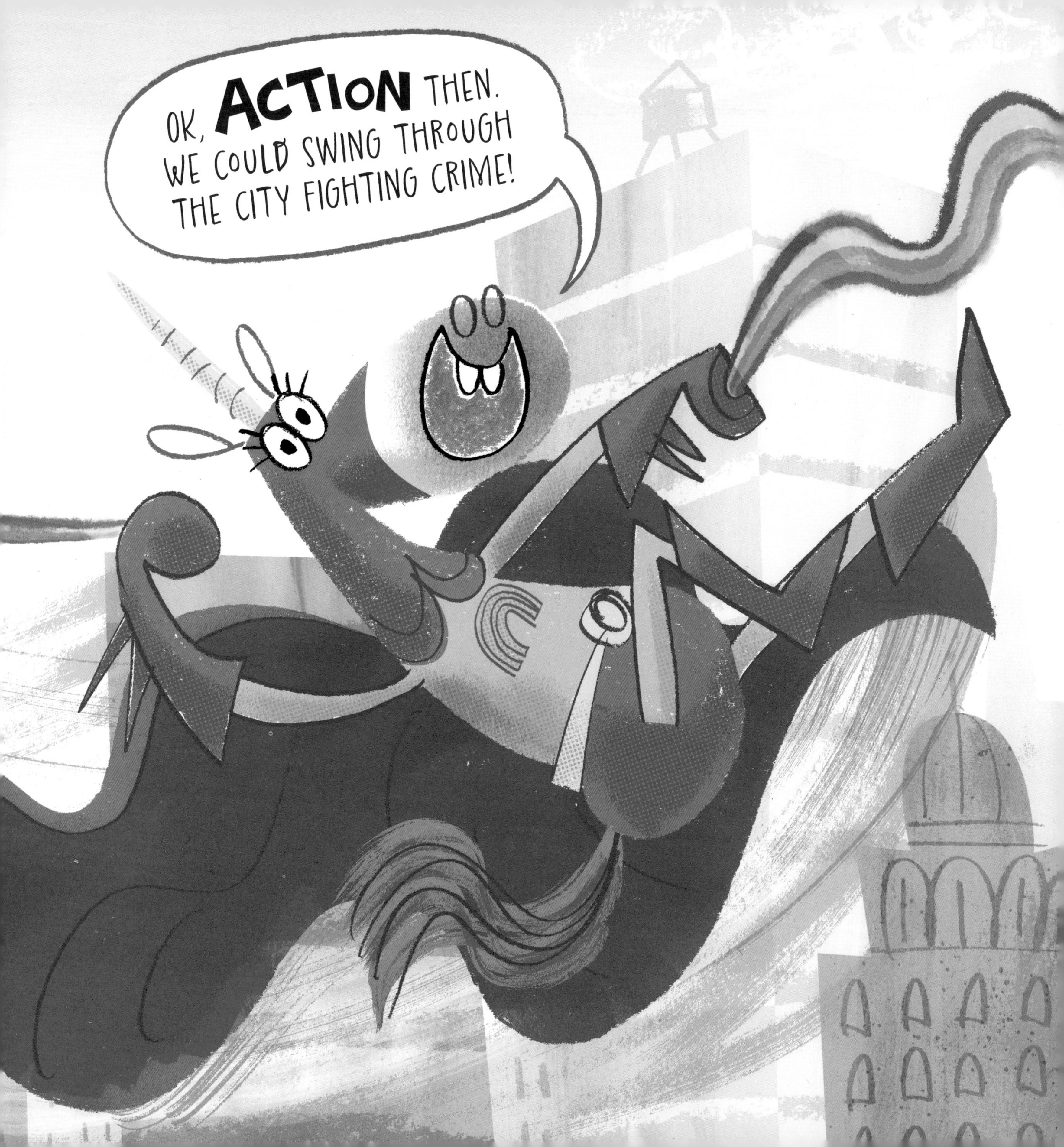
OK, ACTION THEN. WE COULD SWING THROUGH THE CITY FIGHTING CRIME!

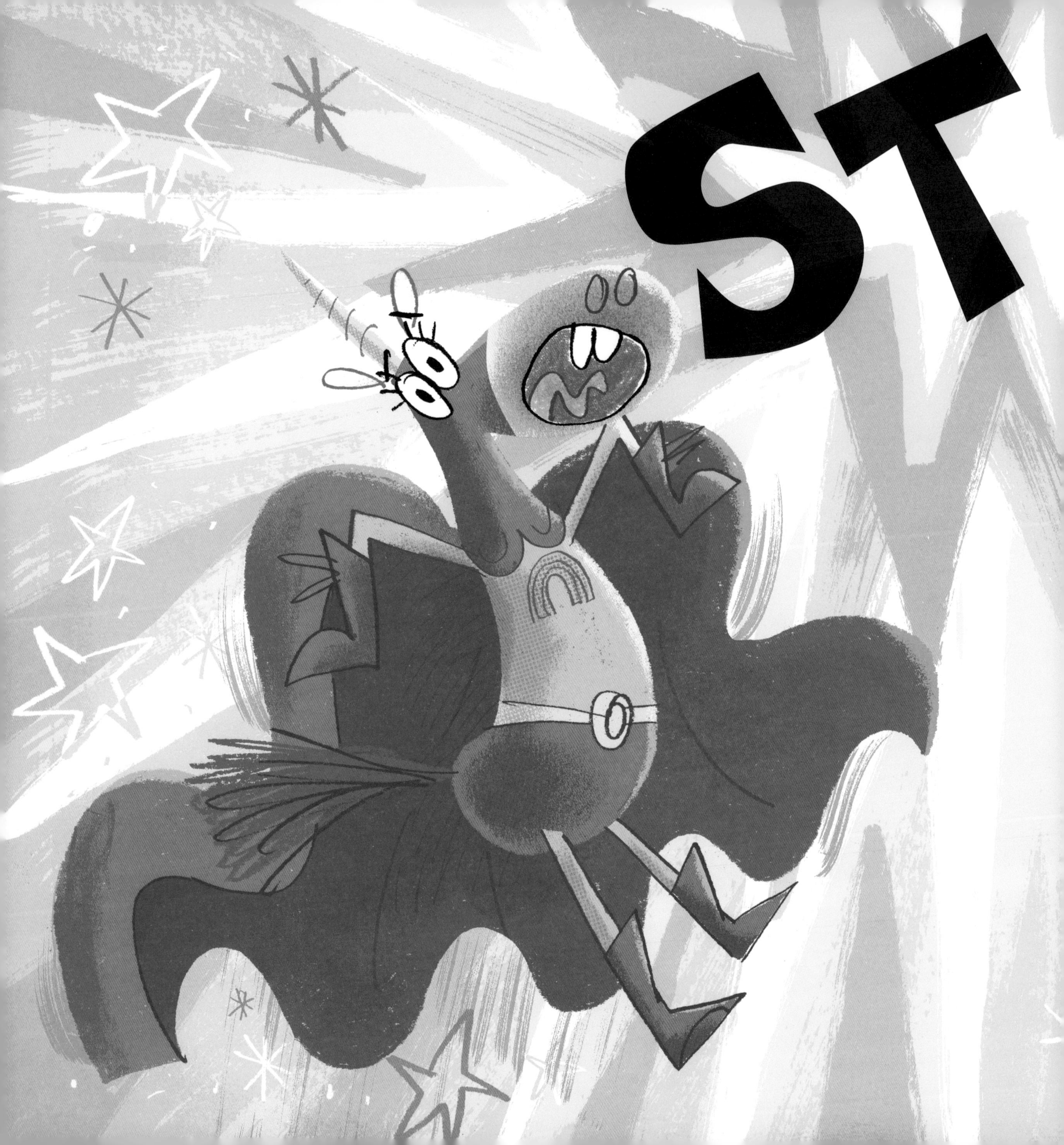
ST

OP!

This is a cowboy story and I'm running out of pages to tell it. There are no PLANES, no WRESTLERS and no SUPERHEROES! Do you understand?

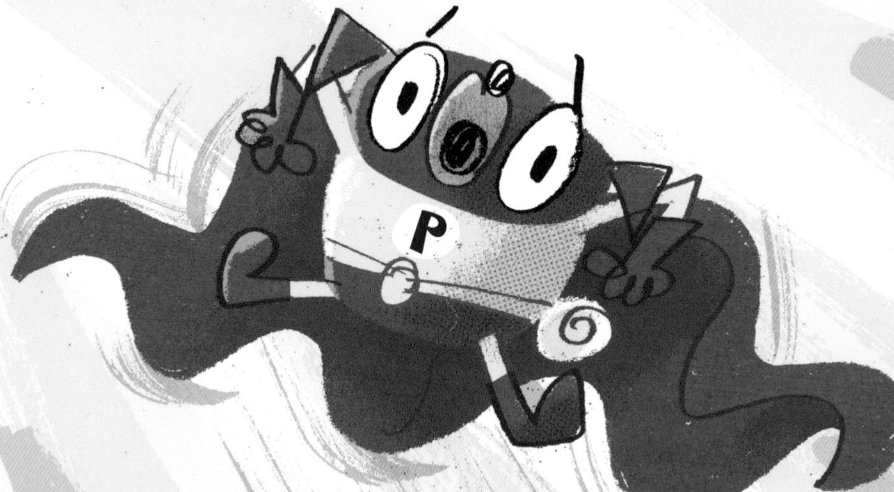
P

I said you can have a <u>small part.</u>
You need to be in the background.

I know! You can be...

... a CACTUS!
There,
now you blend in.

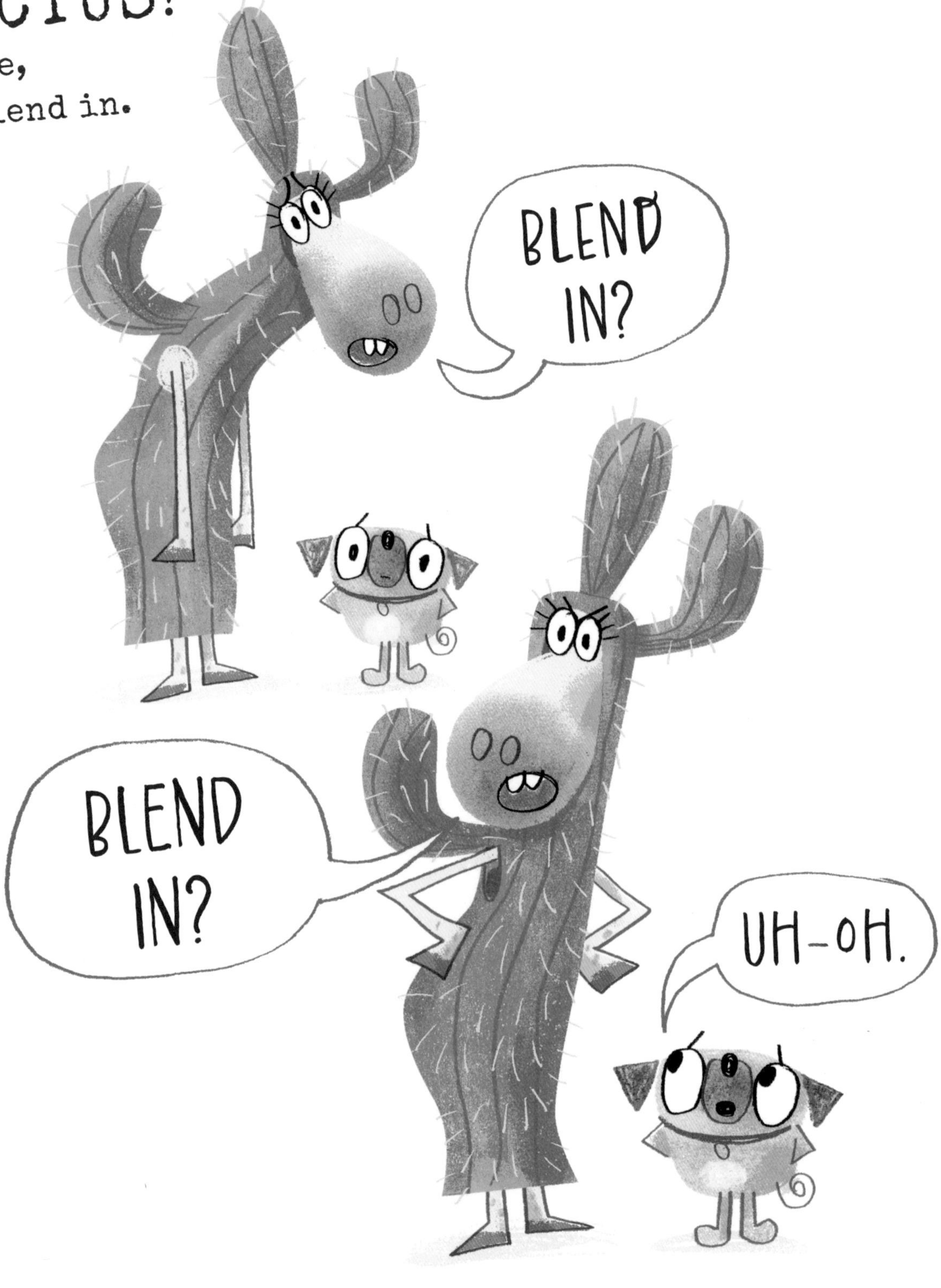
BLEND IN?
BLEND IN?
UH-OH.

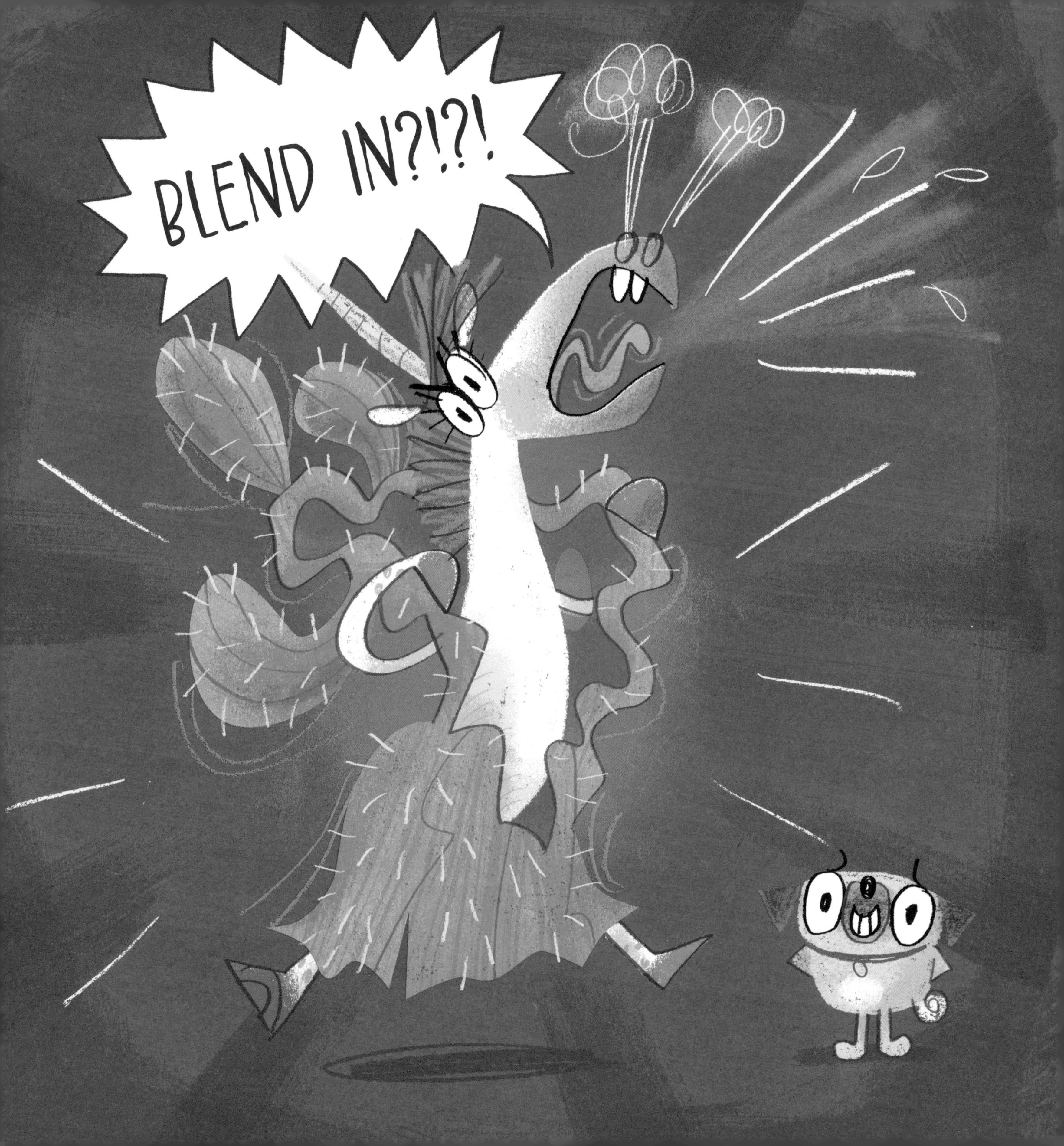
BLEND IN?!?!

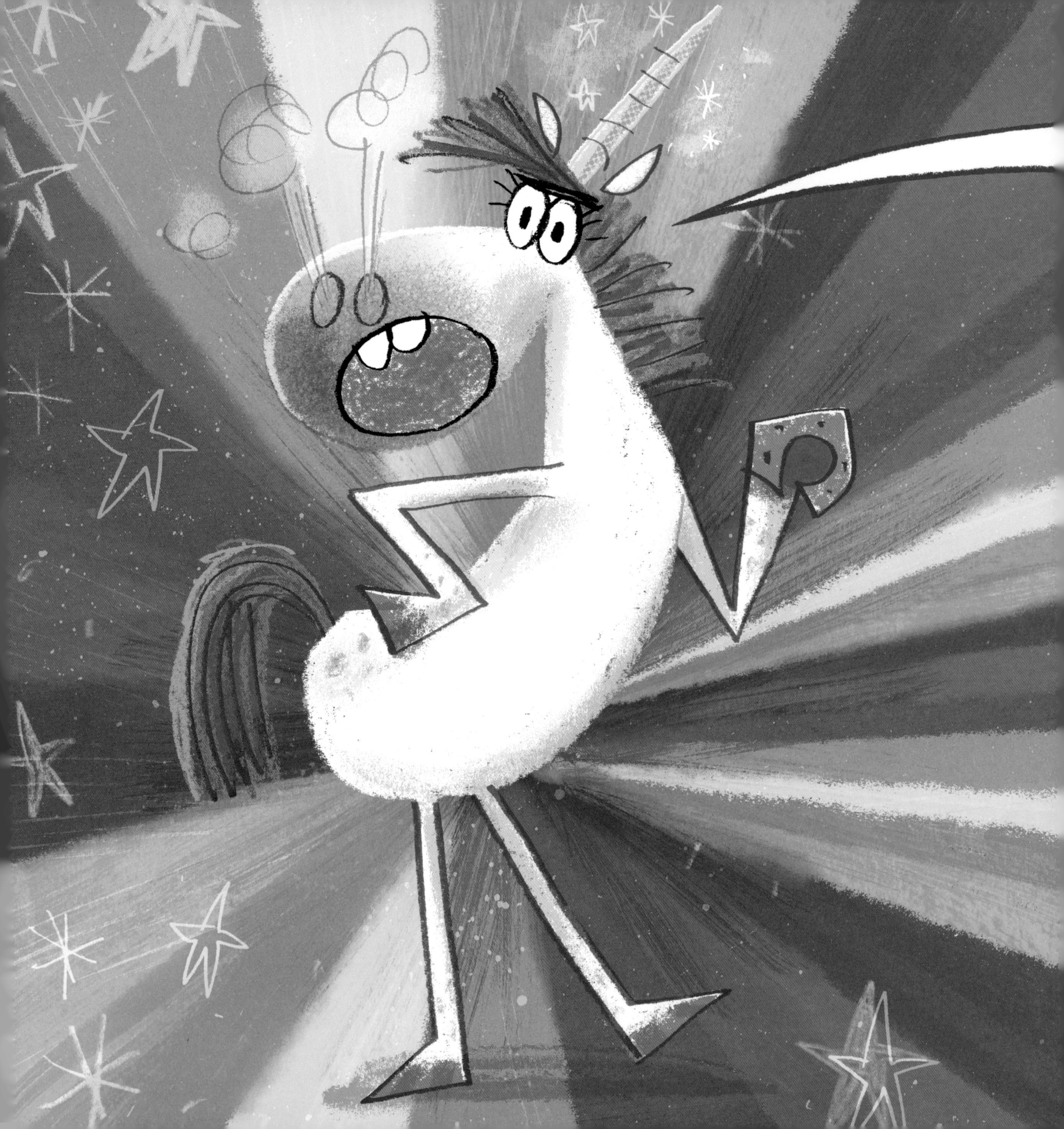

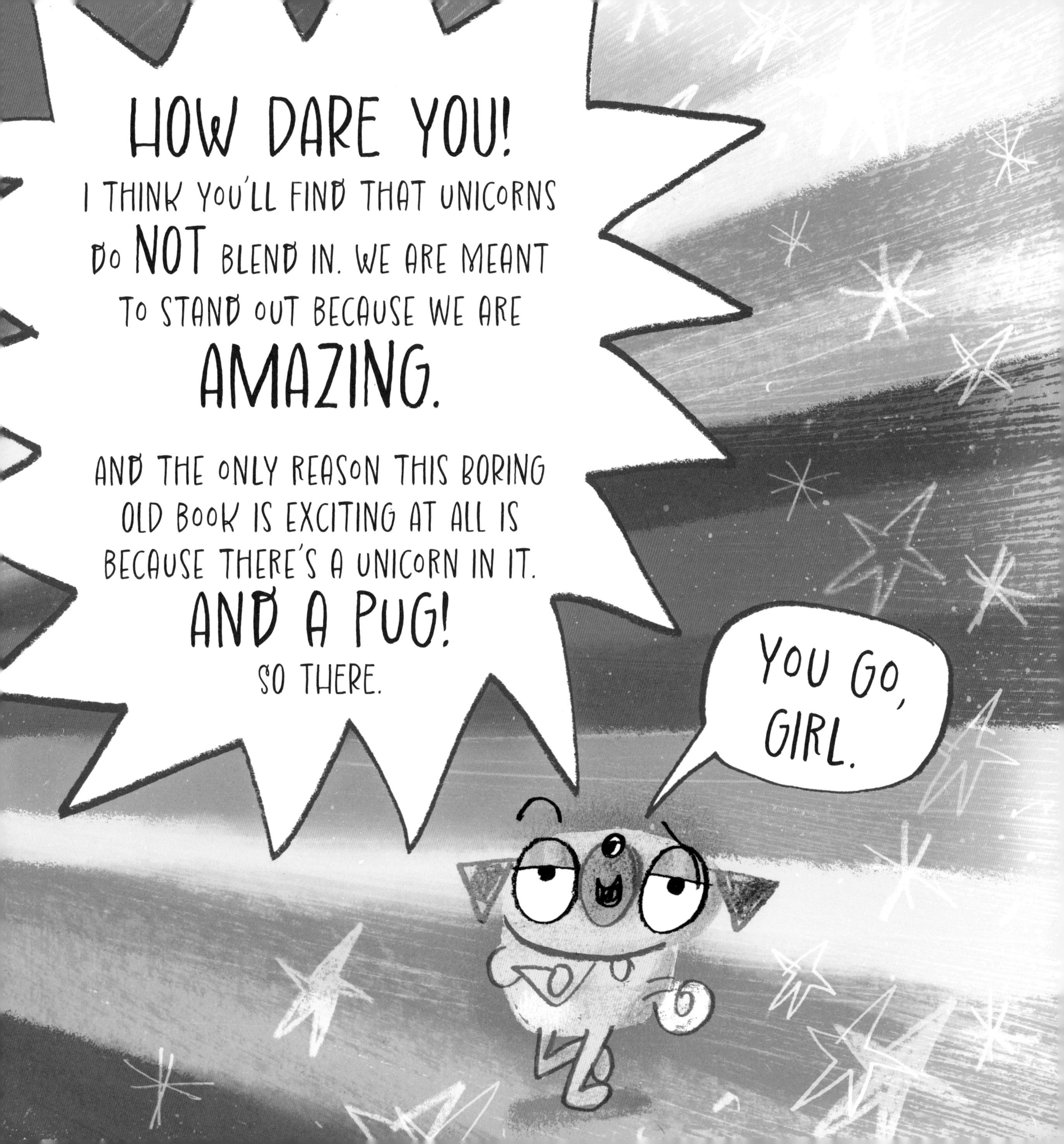
HOW DARE YOU! I THINK YOU'LL FIND THAT UNICORNS DO NOT BLEND IN. WE ARE MEANT TO STAND OUT BECAUSE WE ARE AMAZING.
AND THE ONLY REASON THIS BORING OLD BOOK IS EXCITING AT ALL IS BECAUSE THERE'S A UNICORN IN IT. AND A PUG! SO THERE.
YOU GO, GIRL.

Well, that told us, didn't it?
And it appears we've run out of pages anyway.
So hopefully you enjoyed reading this

unicorn book.

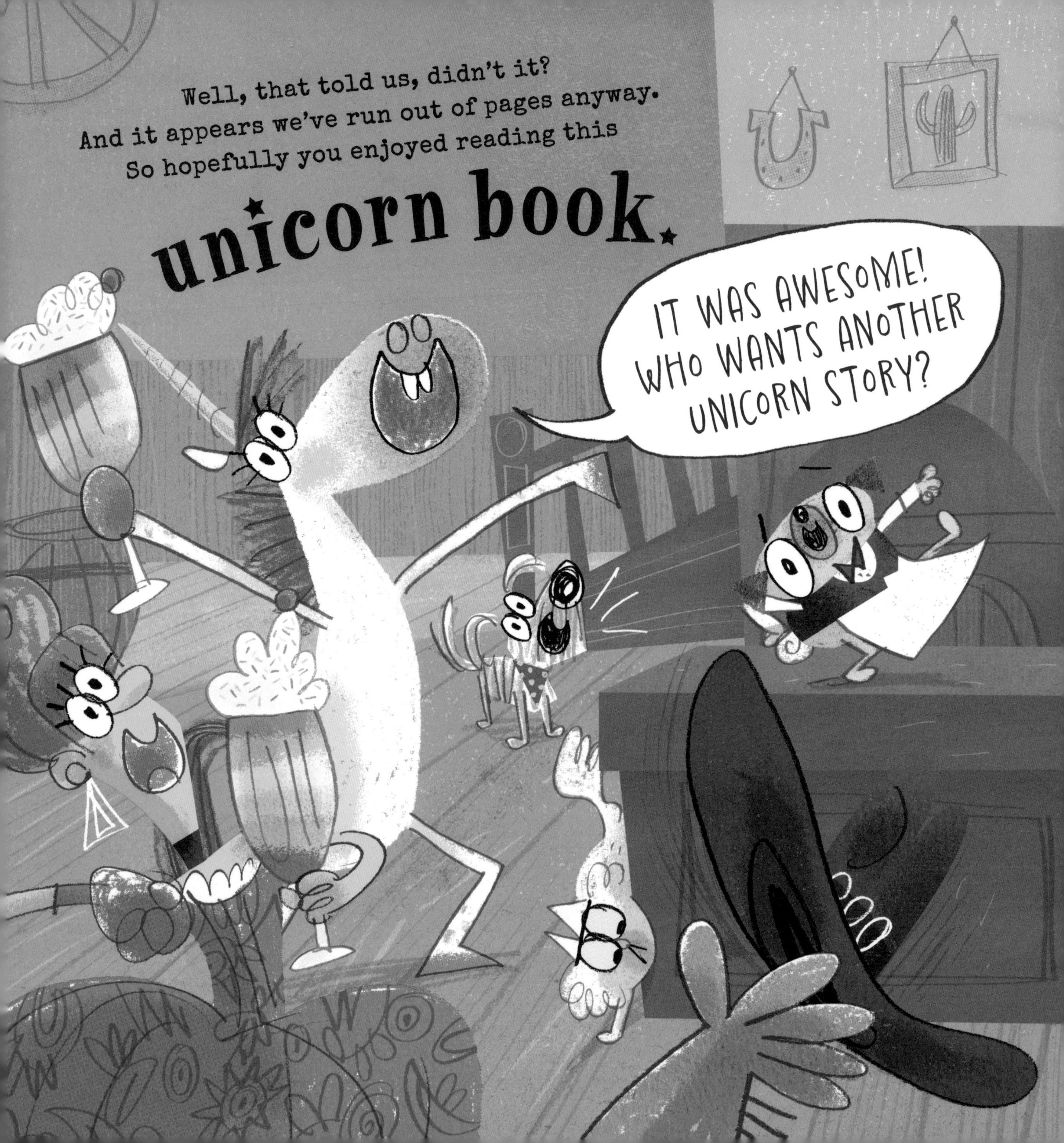
IT WAS AWESOME! WHO WANTS ANOTHER UNICORN STORY?

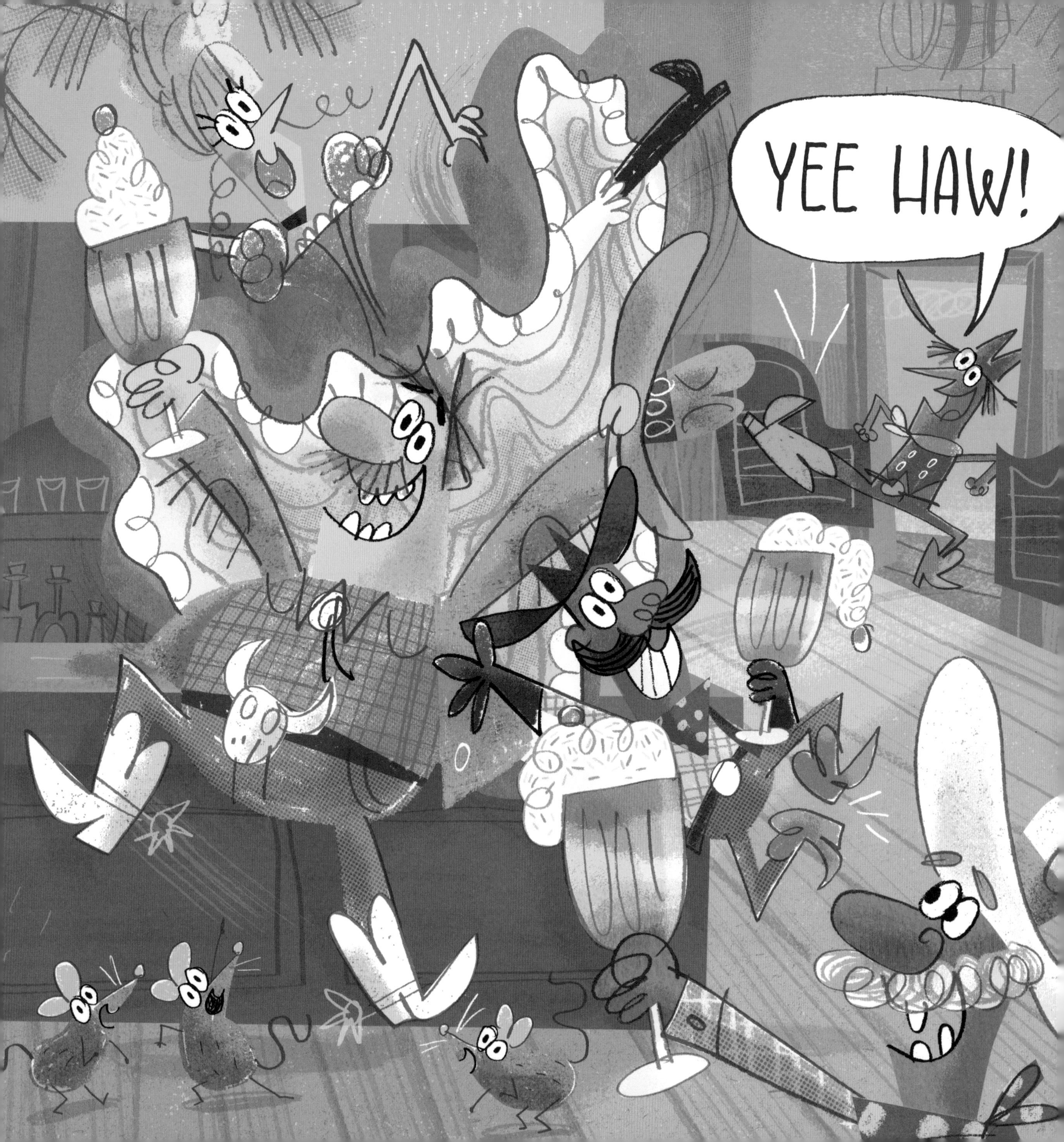
YEE HAW!

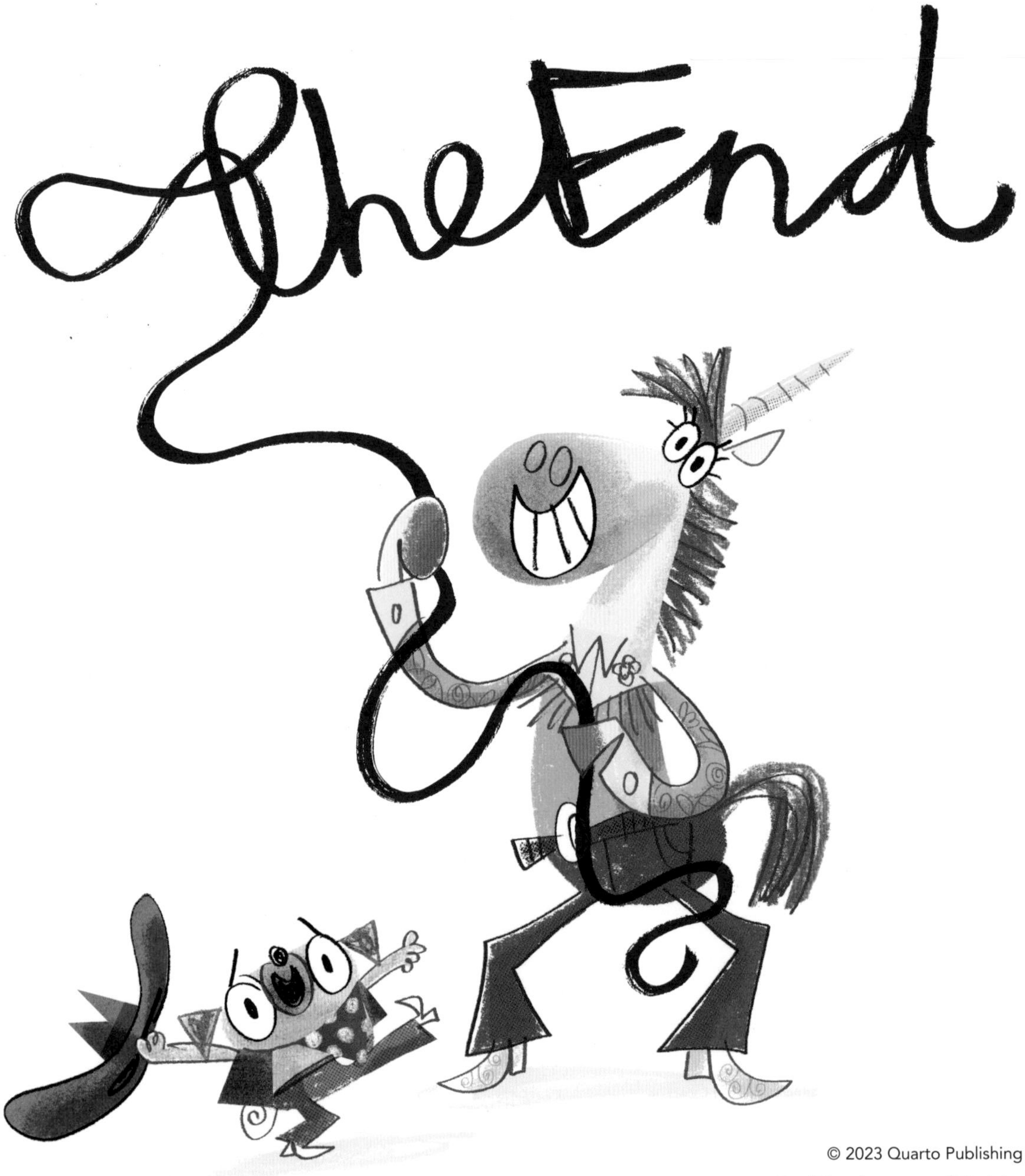
The End

Fred Blunt has asserted his right to be identified as the author and illustrator of this work.

First published in 2023 by Happy Yak, an imprint of The Quarto Group.
100 Cummings Center, Suite 265D, Beverly, MA 01915, USA.
T (978) 282-9590 F (978) 283-2742
www.quarto.com

A CIP record for this book is available from the Library of Congress.

ISBN:978-0-7112-9469-1

FSC www.fsc.org MIX Paper | Supporting responsible forestry FSC® C008047

Manufactured in Guangdong, China CC092023
9 8 7 6 5 4 3 2 1